THE HEART GOES ON

After the death of her husband, financial circumstances force Libby Hargraves to return to work, where she finds that Jack Trennery, the articled clerk she had befriended eight years ago, is now the Melbourne law firm's leading criminal lawyer. But when Jack asks Libby to marry him, she refuses, for he is nine years her junior. But lawyers have a way of getting to the truth, and when Jack is taken hostage Libby has to admit to her true feelings.

KATHY GEORGE

THE HEART GOES ON

Complete and Unabridged

LINFORD
Leicester

First published in Great Britain in 2003

First Linford Edition
published 2004

British Library CIP Data

George, Kathy
    The heart goes on.—Large print ed.—
Linford romance library
    1. Love stories
    2. Large type books
    I. Title
    823.9'2 [F]

ISBN 1–84395–468–0

Published by
F. A. Thorpe (Publishing)
Anstey, Leicestershire

Set by Words & Graphics Ltd.
Anstey, Leicestershire
Printed and bound in Great Britain by
T. J. International Ltd., Padstow, Cornwall

This book is printed on acid-free paper

1

ELIZABETH HARGRAVES, PERSONAL ASSISTANT, the name-plate read. Pausing in the doorway of the familiar office, Libby smiled. The name-plate was a nice touch, but where on earth had Campbell unearthed it from? It stood on her old desk, a little worn around the edges after eight years, not unlike herself, she reflected ruefully.

The connecting door to Campbell's office was ajar, and she caught the murmur of voices behind it as she crossed the room — Campbell's and another, masculine but deeper. She wondered who was with him. Surely it was too early for clients.

Peeling off her jacket, she hung it over the swivel chair, glancing with trepidation at the swish computer. She grimaced. Would she remember anything from the crash course she had done last week?

'Is that you, Libby?'

'Yes,' she replied, her voice a cracked whisper.

She was nervous. She cleared her throat and tried again.

'Yes, it's me.'

'Could you come through, please?' Campbell called.

She tucked a wayward strand of swinging thick hair behind her ear, picked up a pen and pad and pushed on his door. Her first day back was all so familiar and yet so strange.

' 'Morning, Mrs Libby Hargraves!'

Campbell, his face alight, was evidently pleased to have her back.

'Hello, Cam.'

She turned to the stranger and waited to be introduced. A tall man, he was already on his feet.

'You remember Jack, don't you?'

Jack? This was Jack? Of course this was Jack!

The boyish face of the junior articled clerk she had known before had changed into a man's. She did a quick mental calculation. She was thirty-nine this year which would make Jack thirty.

'Libby.'

He leaned towards her and touched his mouth against her cheek. Startled, she caught a tangy smell of clean, fresh man, the smoothness of a shaven jaw.

'Jack,' she murmured.

The structure of the face may have hardened into manhood, but the dark eyes were unchanged. So was the untidy black hair falling over his forehead, contradicting the immaculate image the expensive lawyer's suit projected. Jack never could keep his hair neat.

Campbell cleared his throat. She realised she was staring.

'Jack's going to be handling your case, though I haven't had time to tell him a thing about it.'

'He is?'

Somehow it had never crossed her mind that Campbell would hand her troubles to Jack.

3

'You don't have a problem with that, do you, Libby? I'd like to help.'

Concern creased Jack's brow.

'No, not at all. I'm very grateful.'

'Good. Then I'll see you in my office just as soon as you can drag yourself away from Campbell.'

'When we've cleared up some of this mess, Jack.'

Campbell glanced meaningfully around the room and Libby followed his gaze, taking in the desk, littered with paperwork, then travelling across the floor where files stood in untidy heaps of varying disorder.

'Like next week?' he suggested hopefully.

Jack grinned.

'Sorry, Campbell, but I'd like to see her before then.'

His eyes came to rest on her face. If she wasn't mistaken, this time it was Jack who was staring.

'But right now, I must run.'

He checked his watch, and moved toward the door.

'I'm due in court, the Waterson case,' he said casually.

The Waterson case — of course she'd heard of it. Most people in Melbourne had. A giant construction company was up for fraud and bribery. If Jack was handling the Waterson case he'd moved fast in the years since she'd known him, but then he'd always shown a great deal of promise.

'Nice to see you back, Libby,' he murmured as he passed her.

She tried to find something polite to say but failed. She'd imagined seeing him again countless times but never like this, never him, the lawyer, and she, the client.

'Thanks for waiting, Jack,' Campbell called.

'He waited for me?' she questioned when Jack was out of the office.

'Yes. Seemed quite taken aback when I told him you were returning. Of course, it's none of my business but he'll be late for court now. Quite unlike him.'

Libby sat down in the chair that Jack had vacated. She hoped Campbell would not pursue his curiosity. If he did, she had no idea what she would say. Why had Jack waited to see her?

'So, ready to get stuck in?'

Campbell picked up a file seemingly at random, and she dragged her mind away from Jack and looked around the room again. What a mess! Campbell hadn't been joking when he'd said he couldn't keep a hold on a personal assistant since her departure.

'I feel like I've bitten off more than I can chew,' she said with some apprehension.

'Nonsense! Piece of cake, Libby. You know how I work. You'll have this office and me ship-shape in no time, and as you can see it's high time somebody took me in hand!'

He tilted back in his chair and chewed at the end of his pen.

'So, you approve of me asking Jack to handle your insurance company? He's turned into a fine lawyer. My intuition in selecting him was spot on.'

Libby smiled. As she recalled, it was her intuition back then, but she wasn't about to get into an argument with Campbell on her first day back, however friendly. She needed this job. She'd never regretted choosing Jack from the applicants for articled clerkship. Campbell had needed somebody who was bright, who could think on his feet. Jack Trennery, fresh out of university, had been that somebody.

'Let's get started, Libby,' Campbell interrupted her thought. 'I've got a meeting at two with counsel and a swag of work to get through by then.'

Libby took out her pen and pad and began to write, and before she knew it the morning passed. Time and again she was interrupted by the phone, and old friends on the staff continually popped through the doorway to offer their sympathies and renew their acquaintance.

She made herself a cup of tea in the office kitchenette after lunch, wondering how she had coped with the frenetic pace of a lawyer's office before. Obviously she must have coped very well, so well that Campbell had wanted her back in spite of her skills being out of date.

In hindsight, having a computer at home had been invaluable, enabling her to keep up with changes in technology. Linking up to the internet had been a real challenge, although now Michael knew more about it than she did. He was teaching her — an eight-year-old child!

Returning to her office, tea in hand, she saw Jack come out of her doorway. He stopped when he saw her coming down the passage.

'Would you like a cup?' she asked.

'No, thank you. Campbell in?'

'He's with counsel,' she replied, going into her office. 'He won't be back until four. How did your case go?'

'We've adjourned. The other side produced an unexpected witness.'

Jack shoved his hands impatiently

into the pockets of his trousers.

'What are you really doing here, Libby? You can't need the money, and if you were bored at home, why didn't you tell me you wanted to come back to work? I would have given you a job without any hesitation,' he added.

He took a hand, his left hand, out of his pocket and rubbed at his temple. No wedding band, strange. She was sure he had married, but then not everybody wore a wedding ring.

'It wasn't quite like that, Jack.'

'What? You didn't get tired of playing housewife?'

'No, I didn't.'

'You've changed,' he said unexpectedly, eyeing her through narrowed lids. 'Filled out a bit? It suits you. You were too thin before.'

She laughed self-consciously and sat down.

'That's enough about me, Jack. How have you been?'

'Not bad, in the circumstances.'

'I heard you got married.'

He didn't answer, turned instead to gaze out the window. She frowned. There was something about him she obviously didn't know. Could it possibly be as bad as what had happened to her?

'I can't get used to the idea of you being here,' he said, his voice low.

'You didn't seem to care that much when I left, Jack.'

'You were pregnant,' he said accusingly.

'So? Lots of married women get pregnant. It's perfectly natural. It wasn't like I had a disease or something!'

He crossed to her desk, and gripped the edge.

'You knew I was busy. I had to prove myself to a completely new department,' he said, then took a breath, 'and you knew I had been relying on you. Too much, as it happened.'

She averted her eyes. She knew that. She'd been relying on him, too, relying

10

on his friendship when she had a husband.

'It happened a long time ago, eight years ago,' she said gently. 'It doesn't matter now. Can't we just pick up where we left off?'

He removed his hands from her desk and shook down his jacket sleeves.

'Of course, we can. Would you like to tell me what it is you need a lawyer for? I gather you're in a spot of bother.'

A spot of bother? She'd hardly call it that. Why didn't he know about Simon? Almost everyone else in the office did. It had been front-page news.

'Let me guess, you want me to write a letter about a fencing problem to your neighbour?'

She stared at him

'Jack, it's nothing like that, and if that's your attitude, I'll handle it myself.'

'Don't be ridiculous!'

'Me, ridiculous? What about — '

She stopped herself. They were arguing! They had never argued before.

11

'Why are you so touchy? The Waterson case not going well?'

'As it happens, it's not going according to plan,' he muttered, 'but that's not the point.'

'Like to talk about it?'

'Not really. I don't like discussing death threats at the best of times.'

'Death threats! Jack! When — '

He cut her off.

'I knew I shouldn't tell you, and take that look off your face. I'm a grown man now, not a gawky, articled clerk in need of mothering!'

'No wonder you're upset.'

'I am not upset.'

She bit her tongue. She needed to stay calm. He was going to ask her about Simon in a minute and she would have to tell him.

'I'm waiting,' he murmured.

She had lost track of the conversation. What was he waiting for?

'Has that pilot husband of yours done something he shouldn't have?'

She flushed.

'I'm trying to tell you, Jack. You keep changing the subject.'

'I promise I won't say another word.'

He grinned at her and suddenly he was the Jack of old, the Jack she would entrust with any problem. She rose and walked over to the window, away from his eyes. Far below the towering office, some schoolchildren were playing in the greenery of the Botanic Gardens. In the bright sunlight they looked like tiny beetles in their striped school blazers.

She wondered what Michael was doing. How was being fatherless going to affect his school life? She took a deep breath.

'My husband, Simon,' she began, 'he's . . . he's been killed in a plane crash.'

In the silence, her heart pounded against her ribs, but not from grief. She had no grief for her husband, but there was fear, the fear of being found out she had no grief.

She waited for Jack to offer some caring condolence, for a moment when she could affect wiping her eyes, so that when she turned to him dry-eyed, her composure would appear natural. The silence grew. Curious, she turned towards him.

His mouth hung open, an expression she couldn't fathom on his face. But it was his eyes that puzzled her. They were bright, bright with what? It looked like excitement! It wasn't the reaction she was expecting.

'Why didn't you tell me this before?' Jack demanded.

What a strange thing to say. What had happened to a word like, sorry?

'When have I had time to tell you, Jack? I had absolutely no idea Campbell was going to ask you to handle this for me. He hadn't told me whom he was going to ask. He was to instruct someone before I started work. It was all supposed to be sorted out, pre-arranged.'

'OK, OK, calm down.'

He put up his hands.

'You know what Cam's like with his

14

own staff,' he continued patiently. 'What exactly was he meant to tell me?'

He leaned back against her desk, confident and at ease. Had she imagined that look of excitement in his eyes? She stepped away from the window.

'The airline's insurance company is contesting Simon's life insurance claim. I'm going to have to take them to court. It's a long story.'

'When did this happen?'

'Three months ago.'

'Three months ago I was in Singapore. That's why I know nothing about it,' he said quietly.

Concentration creased his brow, putting two and two together.

'Campbell made you an offer you couldn't refuse — the services of a lawyer in return for recommencing work for him?'

'I had no option, Jack. I can't afford a lawyer.'

The offer Campbell had made her was generous, so generous she couldn't refuse. She was practically penniless and there was Michael to support.

'He missed you, you know.'

'I'm not indispensable.'

She laughed, but it was nervous laughter.

'That's what they all say. Tell me, was that the only reason you came back, to avail yourself of the services of the firm?'

She hesitated. How much information did she give him?

'I need a steady income. I have a child, a mortgage, all the trappings of a middle-aged life.'

'Middle-aged?' Jack snorted. 'There was no other reason? No sentimental grounds? No-one you . . . '

He hesitated as if looking for the right word.

'No-one you missed particularly?'

Puzzled, she drew her eyebrows together.

'What are you on about, Jack Trennery?'

He straightened, and focused his eyes

on some place above her head.

'You'd better come to my office for a consultation tomorrow. I'll go and check my diary now and give you a call to arrange a time. I don't need to tell you to bring all the relevant paperwork.'

He nodded briefly at her and strode curtly out of the room. She frowned and sank into her chair. What had she said to make him leave so abruptly?

She went over her last words. Was it Campbell's offer to return to work? No, there was nothing untoward in that statement. Her brain ticked over, sorting out sentences. He'd made some suggestion, hadn't he, just before he walked out, something along the lines of returning to Williams & Nash because of someone she missed?

She came to a stop. Surely not? Surely he didn't think . . .

Stunned, she broke off the thought, but almost immediately found herself returning to it. He didn't really think she had come back because of him? Shutting the open file on her desk, she

17

strode across the floor to the filing cabinet, jerking out a drawer with a clatter.

Granted, they had been more than work colleagues, but the idea that she might have been sweet on Jack was ridiculous. For goodness' sake, she was nine years older than he was! It was a road she wasn't even going to go down, she thought.

The phone rang as she was tidying her office, readying to leave for home.

'I'm free at four tomorrow, if that time is suitable for you,' the voice said.

'I'll just check with Campbell.'

She left him holding while she talked to her boss then returned to the phone.

'It's fine, thank you, Jack. I'll see you then.'

That night, while Michael started his homework, she found her file containing all the information on Simon's insurance. She picked up a few other papers she thought Jack might need and filed them separately. She didn't want to show them to Jack, but she didn't

18

want to look foolish by not having them with her.

Michael looked up at her as she began to clear away the evening's dishes and pack the dishwasher.

'We've got a new boy in our class.'

'You have? What's his name?'

'Jared. He's got a step-dad. Mum, will I get a step-dad?'

She closed the dishwasher door and wiped her hands.

'It depends who's asking me.'

She smiled down at him.

'If it's Frank, the answer's definitely no.'

Michael giggled. Frank, the next-door neighbour, was over fifty, wore slippers outdoors and fancied her. He came over on the slightest pretext. Last week, he had brought over an open bottle of red wine. He suspected it was off. Could she confirm his opinion?

'Well, what if it's someone who isn't Frank?' he suggested.

Absently, Libby studied his blue eyes and thick straight fair hair. It was uncanny how alike they looked, so much so that someone had recently suggested she was his older sister. She smiled faintly, remembering Michael's hysterical laughter at the time.

'Well? Will I . . . you know . . . get a step-dad?'

'Probably not. Does it matter?'

'Sort of,' he answered. 'I need someone to bowl to me for cricket.'

'You'll just have to make do with me. I'm not that bad, am I?'

Not giving him an opportunity to confirm her suspicion, she went on.

'You can't order instant dads, Mikie. Now, how far are you with your homework?'

She leaned over his head, looking down at his maths. His chances of getting another father were very slim but she didn't want to tell him that. She wasn't gong to marry anyone unless she was completely and utterly convinced they were besotted with her. That was where she had gone wrong with Simon. He hadn't loved her.

But she hadn't known that at the time. In fact, she'd hardly known Simon at all. She'd been swept off her feet by his good looks and confidence. He was older, sophisticated and experienced. He'd overcome all her objections to the rushed marriage and charmed her parents. She'd had no chance to question the rumours about his past. He'd swept them aside with a look and a laugh. What a fool she'd been, a totally gullible, naïve fool.

Now, with the hindsight of maturity and experience, no-one was going to get the better of her or her emotions.

She bit down on her lip. Jack was going to get the better of her emotions tomorrow. She was going to have to tell him a lot of things she'd rather not. Why on earth had Campbell chosen him to take her case? Why couldn't it have been some quiet, obscure senior assistant? She knew the answer.

Jack is a top lawyer; Jack gets things done; no-one messes with Jack. How many times in the years before had

Campbell repeated those phrases to her?

In the morning, she dressed in black tailored trousers and a brightly patterned waistcoat over a soft white shirt. She thought trousers would make a statement, but she wasn't sure what it was she wanted to state.

She was almost late for her appointment with Jack. She was about to leave when Campbell buzzed her for coffee for his clients. He was so inconsiderate sometimes, but she'd worked for him for such a long time before her pregnancy she knew he meant well, even if he was often thoughtless and brusque.

Jack was busy, dictaphone in hand, when she arrived. Wordlessly, he waved her to a chair. She sat down, glancing at the desk which was so different from Campbell's. Pens and pencils sat neatly in a shiny black container, the blotter was squared off to meet the edge of the desk, files sat in an orderly pile on the left side. She smiled inwardly. He might now wear an expensive lawyer's suit, but something about Jack quite clearly had not changed. He clicked off his dictaphone and rose from his chair.

'Sorry,' he said, 'I just had to finish that off. Now, tell me all about this problem with the insurance company.'

She fumbled nervously with her hair, tidying it behind her ear.

'I don't know where to start.'

'At the beginning.'

He began to pace the room.

'Sit down,' she said. 'You're making me feel nervous.'

'Good! I like clients to feel nervous. That way we get straight to the point.'

'But I'm not a client.'

'No, not exactly.'

He perched himself on a corner of his desk, looking at her.

'Just tell me what you told Campbell.'

She took a deep breath.

'Simon was piloting a plane back from Canberra with the Minister of Defence on board.'

He raised his eyebrows.

'The Defence Force's planes were all tied up in an exercise up North,' she explained. 'As Simon taxied into Melbourne, he was warned that an unruly crowd of demonstrators had gathered outside the airport gates. Simon sent word via the flight lieutenant to the Minister, and received a message back, asking him to fly the plane on to Essendon Airport, where the Minister would arrange to be picked up. Of course, Simon cleared the change of plans with the control tower first, and went on to Essendon. The control tower there gave him the OK, but as he came in to land, a small aircraft appeared out of nowhere.'

She paused, then took a deep breath.

'It taxied out directly into the path of the oncoming plane. There was no time. Simon sideswiped it, knocked his own plane off course and headed it straight for the hangar.'

Her heart pounded in her chest again.

'And?'

'Simon and two of the cabin crew were killed, a further seven or eight passengers badly injured. The Minister of Defence escaped with some minor cuts and bruises.'

She remembered vividly when she received the news. She had been distraught, not for herself. She had stopped loving Simon a long time before. It was for Michael. Simon had been his hero. How many boys' fathers were pilots? A week, maybe two, afterwards, she realised she didn't miss Simon at all. She was quite accustomed to managing without him.

Libby looked up at the sound of Jack's voice.

'I'm sorry. What was the question?' she asked softly.

'What's the insurance company's grievance?'

'They're refusing to pay me out.'

She related the gist of several telephone conversations with the insurance company, culminating in her consultation with her head of claims. She'd been informed there would be no payout. The reasons given had been vague, something about an autopsy report, a failure to lodge change-of-flight plans.

'Has the estate been wound up yet?' Jack asked.

'No, it hasn't. I'm the executor.'

'You're the executor? I would have thought that with your efficiency, everything would have been cut and dried by now.'

'I've had a few problems and you know I can't wind things up until all the bills are paid, all the money accounted for.'

'What problems are those?'

'It's complicated, Jack.'

'Why is it complicated? I have to know all the facts.'

Libby pursed her lips. How did she put this?

'There isn't any money to pay the bills, Jack. I desperately need the insurance money.'

'Why don't you have any money?'

She picked up the file on her knees and pushed it across the desk.

'It's we who don't have any money. It's not just me any more, Jack. I have a son, remember?'

'So you do. What's his name?'

'Michael.'

'Libby, pilots of Simon's standing earn a considerable amount. Unless you were living in absolute luxury and frittering it all away, which, quite frankly, I can't see you doing, there must have been savings. What happened to them?'

'It turned out that the fancy sports car I thought belonged to us was on lease,' she explained. 'I sold my little runaround and bought something older and cheaper and that's managed to keep us going for a while.'

'You're not answering my question. What happened to the money?'

She looked away. He wasn't making this easy for her.

'Do you have to know all this? Isn't it

27

sufficient to take my word for it?'

'No, it's not. You know that. Now, if you want me to handle this for you, I need all the facts. You do want me to handle this for you, don't you?'

'I don't have a choice, do I?'

Unable to sit still any longer, she rose suddenly.

'Meaning?'

Why was he making it so difficult for her? And why was she shaking so much? She had never been nervous of him before. She took a deep breath.

'Simon was having affairs. He spent nearly all the money on his . . . '

She hesitated, having difficulty with the words.

'On his women,' she said at last. 'The statements from all his credit cards are all in the file.'

Her hands folded and unfolded agitatedly within each other.

'He went to the races, too, when he was in town.'

'How long had this been going on for?'

'Four or five years, I think. I don't really know.'

She turned to him, blinking away the tears. This time they were real.

'Jack, I don't want anyone to know.'

'You mean no-one knows about this?'

'No. Not his parents, or mine, for that matter. For Michael's sake?'

'You can't be serious.'

'He's . . . he was Michael's hero. Now that he's dead, I can't diminish him in Michael's eyes. Michael wouldn't understand. He's too young. Please, Jack, can we keep this to ourselves?'

'I'll try to, but I can't promise.'

He shook his head as if he was clearing it.

'Whatever possessed him?'

He asked the question softly, as if he was talking to himself, but she answered it. She needed to talk.

'He was that kind of man, a smooth talker, a social creature. He made every woman think she was special. When he married me, he promised it would all stop. For some stupid reason I believed him. If only I hadn't been so naïve!'

'Libby, don't blame yourself. You're only human. We all make mistakes. I did.'

'You did?'

'Yes, but we're not going to talk about me. Go on.'

'There's nothing more to say.'

'Are you sure? You've told me everything?'

She nodded. She wasn't going to tell him she didn't love Simon. He didn't need to know that. She took a quiet, steady breath, clenched her hands into fists and brought herself under control. She took another breath, of fright. Jack was beside her, touching her. Gently, he uncurled her tight fingers.

'You can cry if you want to.'

'I don't want to cry!'

Her voice broke, however, and sobbing, she buried her face in her hands. Jack's arms drew her gently into his warm embrace. He stroked her hair, patted her back.

'Let it all out,' he whispered.

After a minute, he pressed a large white handkerchief into her hand.

'Here, dry your tears.'

She pulled away from him, wiping her eyes.

'I don't know why I'm crying,' she said.

Was it the emotion of putting her husband's sordid life into words?

'It's obvious. You loved him,' he stated matter-of-factly.

She averted her eyes, clasped her hands together, and wondered if he could tell she was lying.

'You did love him, didn't you?'

'He was my husband, Jack.'

'Did you love him?'

'What's that go to do with the insurance claim?'

'It has a lot to do with it, the grief-stricken wife and so on.'

He picked up his pencil and twirled it carelessly between his fingers, as if the question was neither here nor there, but she knew better.

She couldn't tell Jack a lie. It was something she had never done. OK, she told white lies now and again, but this was different. It went against her principles.

'Did you love him?' he persisted.

There was no way out. She knew he would persist until he got an answer, asking the question in a different way if need be. What did it matter if she told him, she thought tiredly. She'd told him everything else, laid bare her life, and lying to her lawyer wouldn't get her anywhere.

'No, Jack, I didn't love him.'

His pencil snapped in two and fell to the ground. Jack made no move to pick up the pieces. He looked like he was in shock.

'I stopped loving him long ago. It was a gradual thing.'

'Why? What did he do to you?'

'I discovered he didn't love me,' she explained. 'I was a trophy wife, something to be admired, but not loved.'

'When did you find that out?'

'Before Michael was born.'

'So you weren't in love with him when I knew you before?'

It was a considered question, but then Jack always thought before he spoke.

'No, not really.'

He swore softly under his breath.

'Why, what does that matter?'

'It doesn't! Forget it!' he cut in.

What had she said to upset him?

'Why did you have a baby if you weren't in love with him?'

She smiled ruefully.

'Silly, wasn't it? At the time I thought it was the right thing to do. He'd always wanted a child, but it only made it worse. I don't know why I was still hanging in there,' she added. 'I guess I was waiting for something that never would happen.'

She glanced at him, but he was staring out the window, miles away.

'What happened to you, Jack?'

He turned at the sound of his name.

'Pardon?'

She could see the question had caught him off guard.

'I said, what happened to you?'

He shook his head.

'This is not the time to talk about me.'

'Why not? I've laid bare my life to you. Surely you can tell me.'

He shook his head again.

'Jack, I know you don't have to tell me, but would you like to? You would have told me before.'

'We were different then.'

'Of course we were different. It doesn't mean we can't talk about things now surely.'

His mouth remained closed in a grim line.

'Jack, I didn't mean to pry. That would have been the last thing on my mind. You know that.'

She moved to the doorway. It was time to go.

'Wait.'

He strode over, stood between her

and the closed door.

'Why do you want to know? What does it matter to you what happened to me? We haven't been in touch for eight years. Why should you suddenly care?'

'I was just interested in finding out how you'd travelled since I saw you last, if you've been happy.'

'Happy?' he questioned with obvious cynicism. 'I've been married and divorced.'

'Divorced?'

She took a step back. Why hadn't anyone told her?

'It didn't work out.'

'Oh, Jack, I'm so sorry.'

'Don't be,' he said. 'I deserve it!'

'How can you say that?'

'I can say it. I deserve it. I've been blind, an idiot!'

'Jack!' she said sharply.

What was the matter with him?

'I think I should go.'

He didn't move, just stood, quietly, arms folded against his chest.

Footsteps came down the passage,

light and quick, and someone knocked. Jack shifted and turned to open the door.

'Is Mr Bailey's new assistant still with you?' an impatient voice came.

'Yes, Jane.'

'Mr Bailey needs her,' the voice insisted.

'We're just finishing up. She'll be along in a minute.'

He turned from the voice and gazed at Libby over his shoulder with dark, troubled eyes. Without thinking, she jerked the door out of Jack's grasp.

'I'm ready to go, now.'

Ducking her head underneath his arm, she fled down the passage.

2

Someone knocked at Libby's front door at the weekend, when she least expected anyone. Only minutes before, she had returned from the gym, and Michael was still at cricket. In the boy's absence, Puddles, the dog, went berserk with hysterical barking. Grabbing hold of the golden retriever's collar, she opened the door.

The man on the step had on a white drill shirt. His long legs were covered in faded blue jeans and he wore work boots on his feet. He had dark brown eyes and unkempt hair. It was none other than Jack! She took a breath. She'd never seen him in anything but a suit. But what was he doing on her doorstep?

Puddles jerked himself out of her numb fingers and sniffed with excitement around Jack's footwear.

'He's smelling the farm dogs,' Jack explained.

'The what?'

'Farm dogs. That's where I should be, at the farm.'

He fingered the dog's ears as the retriever gently licked his wrist.

'Are you going running?'

She looked down at herself in her runners, bare legs, baggy T-shirt. She ran her hand through her hair. She wasn't quite in the attire to greet your lawyer in.

'I've just got back from the gym.'

She swung the towel off her neck and wiped her face.

'May I come in?'

The hint of amusement in his voice was unmistakeable.

'Of course,' she replied and widened the door.

'I left a message on your answering machine,' he said as he followed her down the passage.

Messages were usually from her mother. They were very close and it wasn't unusual for them to talk every day. It hadn't always been that way but Michael's birth had drawn them together.

'I haven't had time to listen yet,' she said over her shoulder. 'I've literally just walked in the door.'

She led the way into the kitchen. He stopped at the French doors and looked out at the back garden. She remembered that he hated being caged in. It was something to do with being born in the country and living on a farm all his childhood. She unlocked the doors and swung them open, letting in the warm, summer air. He went down the steps into her garden.

Taking a jug of water out of the fridge and two glasses from the cupboard, she joined him outside.

'I've been cutting back the bougainvillaea this morning,' she explained, indicating the heap of cuttings.

He surveyed the creeper climbing the garage wall.

'Where're the secateurs? You missed a bit.'

She passed him the gardening tool and watched as he reached up and expertly cut back here and there. He'd obviously had some experience.

'Where do these go?' he asked, putting down the secateurs and picking up the bundle of clippings.

'Oh, Jack,' she remonstrated, 'I can do that later.'

'I said, where do they go?'

She gave up.

'Around the corner, in the garbage bin. I don't compost them because they're so thorny.'

In a couple of minutes, he had removed the unsightly pile.

'Now you can see the petunias,' he said and pointed out the terracotta pots of colour. 'Pretty, aren't they? Your son, does he look like you?'

'He'll be back from cricket soon and you can see for yourself,' she answered lightly. 'You'd better tell me what you're here for,' she went on, 'because you won't get much of a chance once he finds out you can throw a ball.'

'I made the high school cricket team, if that counts.'

'That'll impress him, though he'll talk you into cricket even if you just throw, like I do, and, failing that, he'll go on for hours about science fiction. I'm afraid he inherited Simon's way with words.'

She gulped at her water, wishing suddenly she hadn't mentioned Simon.

'So, why the visit?'

'Do I have to have a reason? Are you going to throw me out if I haven't?'

She smiled. This was more like the Jack she knew.

'Why else would you come?'

'Maybe I just wanted to see you.'

Fingers moved up and down her spine. She laughed awkwardly.

'Come off it, Jack. What would you want to see me for? I'm older than you, financially destitute and a single mother.'

'So?'

Libby had no answer. The silence grew. She had a feeling that something

41

of importance had been said, that he had set a trap for her into which she had uncomprehendingly fallen.

'But you're quite right, I do have a reason,' he said at last, rescuing her. 'I need help. I've got some advice that has to be out by Monday. I was hoping you could be that help.'

'I'm happy to help you out, Jack, but why me? Surely Jane would have been a better choice.'

'I thought it would be a good opportunity for us to discuss your case, go over any queries you might have.'

Put like that, how could she say no? She opened her mouth but the sudden noise of the dog barking and the front door slamming drowned out any argument she might have made.

'I'm home, Mum!'

Michael burst out on to the patio, then pulled up short.

'Sorry, Mum, I didn't know — '

'Michael, this is Mr Trennery,' Libby said.

'Jack,' Jack said, holding out his hand

for the boy to shake, which he did somewhat gingerly.

'How was your cricket, sweetheart?' Libby asked.

'Great! Can I have a drink? They were fifty-three not out and I clean-bowled one of them. Is there anything to eat?'

He paused while he took the glass Libby gave him.

'Wait on, I mustn't eat too much. We're going out for lunch, aren't we?'

Libby placed her hands on Michael's shoulders.

'Mr Trennery, Jack, works at the same firm where I do. He needs me to go into the office to do some work today.'

'Do you have to? You promised.'

Crestfallen, Michael stole a sideways look at Jack. Jack scratched his forehead thoughtfully.

'I think, at a push, we might just be able to fit in a burger.'

'Cool!' her son said. 'Does that mean I get to come with you?'

'You'll have to bring something to keep you busy while your mother and I work.'

'I've got a computer game and I've got a book.'

'I'll shower and change quickly,' Libby interrupted, glad of an excuse to get out of her sweaty clothing. 'Show Jack your tomato plants while you wait,' she called out over her shoulder, but there was no need to give them a topic of conversation.

As she headed for the bathroom, she heard Michael say, 'Jack, can you play cricket?'

They set off in Jack's open-top car. As soon as Libby saw it she knew her chances of persuading Michael to go in her old model were pretty awful. But she had to go back inside the house and get a scarf for her hair. She sat in the back, relieved she had worn jeans and a tailored shirt and not a skirt which might have blown up around her waist! She wanted Michael to enjoy the thrill of being in the front seat where all the action took place.

Somewhere en route to the office, she glanced into the rear-view mirror and made contact with Jack's dark eyes. She smiled and a happy grin broke out across his face. The eyes held hers.

Why was he staring at her? Was her mascara smudged? She lowered her face, ran her fingers under her eye-lashes. There was a sudden sharp squeal of brakes as the car came to an abrupt halt. She lurched forward in her seat, the vehicle in front of them uncomfortably close.

'Wow!'

Michael sniffed the air and caught the smell of burning rubber, suitably impressed.

'What happened?'

'I wasn't watching the road, was I?'

Libby suppressed a giggle and gazed out of her side window. Two girls in the vehicle alongside were staring. She wasn't sure what was attracting them more, the car or the man.

Jack took Michael for a burger while

she made a start on the advice, and by the time they returned she was more than halfway through. From the colour on their faces they had stopped at the park, presumably to play more cricket. They brought her a soft drink and a cold hamburger which Jack heated up in the kitchenette. Hamburgers weren't her favourite food, but she was very hungry and ate without tasting.

Michael sprawled over a sofa in Reception with his latest Harry Potter book and began to read. Jack took a chair near her desk and started to go through the work.

Out of the corner of her eye, she could see his long legs stretched out in front of him. A small tear in his jeans needed fixing. She wondered who mended his clothes, or did the tear indicate that he lived alone, that he was not currently involved with anyone?

On the computer screen, two documents appeared, one after the other. She frowned, muttered under her breath. What did Jack's private life have to do with her! He lifted his head.

'Am I disturbing you?'

'No, not at all.'

She was telling a lie, a white lie, but still a lie. He was disturbing her, but why?

It was after four when she finished. Feeling pleasantly tired, she left the last pages printing while she checked on Michael. He was playing solitaire on Jack's laptop.

'Did you have a good time?' she asked quietly, stretching her stiff limbs.

'Oh, yes,' he replied, not taking his eyes from the screen. 'He sure can bowl, Mum.'

Jack had made himself comfortable in her office when she returned, thrown his legs up on her desk.

'Would you like a cup of coffee?'

He looked up at her.

'Pardon? I'm sorry, I was miles away. Bad habit.'

'Don't worry, we all have plenty of those.'

'You have bad habits? Name me one.'

He put his hands up behind his head and stretched, seemingly pleased by the interruption.

'I've picked the wrong man to fall in love with more than once.'

She felt the blood drain from her face. Why on earth had she said that? It had nothing to do with anything! Certainly nothing to do with Jack!

'Forget I said that. I must be tired. It was silly.'

'You obviously said it for a reason.'

'I said it without thinking, Jack. Let's talk about something else.'

'I like this topic. How many wrong men have there been?'

'There was someone before Simon, that's all. I was very young.'

'What happened?'

'I got hurt, of course.'

'Oh, Libby,' he said gently, obvious concern in his voice and his eyes. A big lump formed in her throat. She swallowed.

'About that coffee, would you like some?' she said a little too briskly.

'Yes, please.'

'Black, no sugar, right?' she went on.

'Your memory's good,' he replied, as she busied herself. 'Do you think you'll marry again? Third time lucky, maybe?' he asked when she returned with his coffee.

'There will be no third time and no maybe,' she answered firmly. 'Don't you have some corrections for me?' she asked, changing the subject.

'Yes, I do, all of my own doing. You haven't lost your touch. Campbell's a lucky man.'

He rose and gave her the paperwork.

'How can you be so sure you won't marry again?' he asked.

She sank into the chair, glad of its support. She had forgotten how persistent Jack could be, and all this talk about marriage was making her nervous. Surely he could sense she didn't like talking about her private life.

'Why do we keep talking about me, Jack?'

'Just answer the question.'

'Why? I'm not in the witness box, am I?'

Her answer raised a smile and no further comment, but he didn't go away. He picked up his coffee and sipped at it, watching her. She shuffled the papers on her desk, clicked the computer mouse and found the place on her screen.

'When you get all this insurance money, you'll need to be careful.'

She raised her eyes from her work, wishing he would go away.

'Careful of what?'

'Careful of unscrupulous goldiggers.'

'Oh, please, Jack, as if . . . '

From what she had heard, single men, unscrupulous or otherwise, were a scarcity. He put his coffee cup down and leaned towards her.

'Didn't anyone ever tell you how attractive you are?'

Her hands on the edge of the desk began to tremble. She closed her eyes, opened them again, concentrating on the screen in front of her, not seeing any of the words.

'Several times,' she said shakily. 'It was the only thing Simon ever said to me. He wouldn't touch me for months, but he would always tell me how beautiful I was. Now, please let me get on with my work, Jack,' she whispered.

It was almost dark before the advice was e-mailed to Jack's client. They locked up and went down to the building's front entrance. Michael raced ahead, happy to be out of the office. If there was a silence between them, it was the comfortable, relaxed one of the satisfaction of a good day's work.

'Here are the car keys. Would you like to drive?'

Jack dangled them temptingly in front of her. She hesitated. It was such a beautiful car. How could he trust her with it?

'Go on,' he urged. 'I know you'd love to.'

'How did you know?' she whispered. 'Ah-ha!'

He opened the driver's side and she

slid on to the plush leather upholstery.

'Just one thing,' he whispered in her ear, 'a small thing but important. If you get a speeding fine, it's all yours.'

As he drew back, his hair brushed against her cheek. She turned to smile, but a movement behind him caught her eye. In the fading light, someone was closing in on Jack from behind, too fast for a casual encounter. She saw something in the assailant's hand, something raised to strike. She called out a warning, but it was too late, as Jack shut the car door on her words.

She heard the sharp crack of the implement hitting home, followed by a groan. A thud followed as Jack's body fell heavily against the side of the car. Libby drew breath and screamed.

3

Libby got the door open as fast as possible. Jack lay face down in the road. She stepped over his body and located his wrist. His pulse was steady and her sigh of relief was audible.

'Mum, is he going to be all right?' Michael asked, concern in his voice, and something else — fear.

'I don't know. Can you help me get him off the road?'

Together they turned Jack's body over, then half-lifted, half-dragged him to the pavement. It wasn't easy. She put her hand under his head and turned it, so she could make out the wound on the right side. It oozed with blood.

'If he doesn't come to soon, we'll have to get an ambulance. Could you go and see if there's any water in the car, please, Mike? Jack, wake up!'

He groaned, moving his head slowly

and at last opened his eyes. With difficulty, he pulled himself up, leaning on one elbow.

'Jack, are you OK?'

He grimaced. Was he in too much pain to speak? She tried again.

'Jack, does it hurt much?'

'It hurts,' he stated, wincing. 'Did you see who did it?'

'Dark hair, unshaven, stocky.'

It was the best she could do as it had been almost dark.

'I've found some water,' Michael announced at her elbow.

'Good boy. Jack, can you get up?'

Jack rose and walked shakily to a nearby bench under a street lamp. He sat down heavily and spoke again.

'Michael, in the glove box there's a small silver flask. Could you bring that to me, please?'

Libby took out a tissue, wet it with water and wiped away the blood trickling down his face. The street light was dismal, but the wound looked worse than she had anticipated.

'Ouch,' he exclaimed.

'Sorry,' she said. 'I'm trying to be gentle. It must have been a planned attack. Your wallet's not been taken. Why would anyone do this to you?'

'Oh, I don't know,' he replied off-handedly. 'Probably some thug who wasn't happy with his sentence, thought I could have negotiated a better deal. I've had threats before. I don't take them seriously.'

Michael appeared with the flask. Jack unscrewed it and took a swig.

'Thanks, Mike.'

He offered the flask to Libby.

'Whisky?'

'No, thank you. Let's hope that's the end of your thug.'

'Somehow I doubt it,' he said tiredly. 'I think that's the beginning.'

'What do you mean?'

'I think he's going to give me a bashing for every year he spent in jail. I'm probably due another one.'

'Oh, Jack.'

She leaned down and kissed him

lightly on his cheek, suddenly all motherly softness and concern. He squinted up at her.

'Actually, I think it was ten years he spent inside.'

Ten more bashings! Aghast, she stared at him, but the corners of his mouth twitched. He was having her on!

'This isn't funny, Jack.'

'I just want another kiss.'

'Let's get home where I can see to this wound properly,' she said primly, taking his arm. 'You may need stitches.'

He eased himself into the car, waving away her concern.

'I'm OK,' he said grim-voiced, leaning back gingerly against the headrest and closing his eyes.

She drove carefully, but the journey seemed to take for ever. At last she pulled up outside her house.

'Michael, will you please go and unlock the front door and feed Puddles? He'll be almost frantic by now.'

She handed him the keys, and he

took them wordlessly from her.

'You OK, Mike?'

The boy had been silent on the way home. Had the night's events frightened and confused him?

'Yep, I'm OK,' he replied and ran towards the door.

'Good.'

She shook Jack gently.

'Jack we're home.'

'We are?' he said groggily, opening one eye. 'I don't suppose I'm going to get out of this examination. Where do you want me to go?'

'The kitchen will be fine.'

She grabbed some cottonwool and antiseptic in the bathroom, and ran her fingers absentmindedly through her hair. She looked a mess, but this was no time to worry about her looks. In the kitchen, Jack leaned back in a chair, his eyes closed. Libby filled a bowl with warm water and got to work.

Nursing had been her chosen career. She'd spent three months at it and gone through several boxes of tissues before she decided she and nursing were incompatible.

She dabbed at Jack's head, making little progress. He had too much hair, vast amounts of the stuff. It was no wonder he couldn't keep it neat. She opened a drawer and drew out the kitchen scissors.

'What're you doing?' he asked.

'I'm sorry, Jack. I don't like doing this, but I'm going to have to cut some of your hair.'

The area cleared, she set to work again. A moment later, he flinched.

'Sorry, splinters,' she explained.

She put the lid back on the bottle of antiseptic, pushed a piece of her own wayward hair behind her ear and said, 'Right, hospital. The skin's been split by the impact of the blow and I want an opinion on stitches. You also need a tetanus shot.'

'Not really?' he grumbled.

'Yes, really. Who knows where that wood's been?'

They had a long wait at the hospital.

It was Saturday night and there were far more serious cases than Jack's, but at last a nurse led them into a curtained cubicle. She studied Jack's head, then took a razor to his scalp and shaved the area around the wound. Libby wondered why she had been the least bit worried about cutting his hair earlier!

Five minutes later a doctor came in and, after a brief examination, began to stitch Jack up. Glancing at Libby, he smiled knowingly.

'You won't notice the scar now, but one day when he's balding, you'll be grateful.'

The doctor assumed she was Jack's wife!

'I'm not . . . er . . . we're not . . . um . . . '

'Oh,' the doctor said, raising his eyebrows, surveying Libby over his patient's head.

'Well, if I was you, mate, I'd do something about it,' he said conversationally.

Jack grunted. Flushing, Libby occupied her mind by imagining what Jack would look like when he was sixty and balding! With all that hair, she concluded, it was doubtful he would ever go bald.

'You'll have to stay the night with us,' she told him as they led a very sleepy Michael back to the car.

'Taking the doctor's suggestion to heart, I see,' Jack murmured.

'Absolutely not! How could you think such a thing! Someone needs to keep an eye on you, that's all.'

'That's all?' Jack said with a smirk.

Scarlet-faced, Libby ignored him.

Back home, she put out a new toothbrush and toothpaste for him, went through to the spare bedroom and pulled back the coverlet. The linen had been changed a week ago when her mother had stayed overnight.

'I could get used to this,' was all he said when she took him to the room.

★ ★ ★

60

Returning from her lunch break, Libby entered a vacant lift and pressed the button. As the doors closed, a hand came between them, jerking them to a halt. She looked up in alarm.

'G'day.'

'Jack!'

Gone was the tousled, overlong look. His hair had been cut short.

'You didn't have to cut it, did you?' she protested, resisting the temptation to run her hand over it.

'I could hardly go around looking like I'd been tomahawked by Mohicans, could I?'

'I don't know, Jack. Lots of people have weird haircuts,' she answered, brushing snippets of hair off his jacket.

'Yeah,' he growled. 'Hoodlums maybe, but not lawyers! Between you and that nurse, I've been fair savaged!'

To her horror, Libby felt a giggle beginning. She turned away and tried valiantly to straighten her face. Pursing her lips, she brought herself to look at him a second time. His eyes flickered

61

with amusement, surprising her.

'You haven't really changed at all, have you? I suppose I'll have to concede defeat and admit that's one up to you. But, if I remember correctly, you've got a lot of catching up to do.'

'Says who?' She changed the subject. 'How is your head?'

He lowered it in reply. Without thinking she put out a hand to touch, then withdrew it quickly.

'It's OK, you can touch. It's numb,' he said.

'Numb?'

She fingered the short bristles of hair, marvelling at the neat stitches.

'The nerve endings have been damaged. Apparently it can take up to six months for the feeling to return.'

The lift slowed, bouncing to a gentle halt.

'Don't go,' Jack said abruptly. 'We need to talk.'

He pressed the ground-floor button without waiting for her answer.

'Jack! We could've talked out there.'

'No, we couldn't. People will talk about us talking.'

'You're my lawyer. I'm entitled to talk to you.'

'This is not strictly talking, this is inviting. I want you to come to dinner. I've had a reply from the insurance company.'

'What did it say?'

'It says you must come to dinner.'

'Jack, be serious!' she hissed.

'I am!'

The lift shuddered. Libby's gaze flew to the numbers lit up above the door. They had returned to the ground floor! She looked at Jack helplessly as the doors opened. People they both knew waited in the foyer. She emerged and nodded her greetings then made her way toward the second set of lifts around the corner, wondering if Jack would have the same idea.

'Do you see why you need to come to dinner?' his voice murmured over her shoulder.

She half-turned, her eyes making

contact with a charcoal pin-stripe suit. He stood behind her, so close she could count the small dark freckles at the side of his nose. There were five, or was it four?

'No, I don't,' she said crossly. 'This is silly. Why can't I just come up to your office for a consultation?'

'Because, you didn't call the lift.'

'The lift?'

She gazed at the buttons blankly.

'No, I didn't. I'm . . . I'm . . . '

He leaned a long arm over her shoulder and did it for her.

Flustered, was what she wanted to say. She never got flustered. It was a trait her boss admired in her.

'You're flustered,' he filled in as if he understood her state of mind perfectly.

Footsteps approached.

'Blast!' Jack murmured. 'So, dinner, tonight?' he went on in a rush. 'Shall we say seven-thirty, my place? You remember where I live?'

She nodded and then Jack drew back

putting a respectful distance between them.

'Hello, you two!'

'Hello, Bill,' Jack responded.

Libby turned. It was Mr Williams, one of the founder partners of the firm. She put aside her anxiety and smiled warmly at him.

'You keeping this young whipper-snapper in line, Libby?' he asked.

'No, I'm not having any success, Mr Williams. What do you suggest?'

She glanced at Jack, hoping to see a smidgen of humility, but instead he beamed with triumph. What was going on?

4

'Nice outfit,' her sister, Ruth, complimented, circling Libby with critical eyes.

'Oh, this is old,' Libby said.

She pulled at the hem of the sleeveless powder-blue dress, straightening it, and rearranged the folds of the soft white pashmina over her bare shoulders. It had taken three changes of clothing to dress for dinner with Jack, but she wasn't going to tell Ruth.

'You look stunning,' her sister admitted grudgingly, 'but then you always do. Who is this man?'

'He's just my lawyer,' Libby said indifferently.

'Your lawyer?' Ruth's eyebrows rose.

'There are some complications in the will,' Libby said, plumping up cushions on the sofa — it wasn't a lie.

'I've left you some chocolate tea to

have with your cake,' she continued, 'and Michael — '

'Chocolate tea?' Ruth interrupted.

'I mean, oh, Ruth, you know what I mean!'

'The lady is nervous,' Ruth murmured.

Libby grimaced. Had she really said chocolate tea?

'I expect you'll be home early then, if he's just your lawyer?'

Ruth's career as a journalist trained her to be persistent.

'I expect I will be, but don't panic if I'm not.'

'Hi, Mikie,' Ruth said to the slightly pink and damp boy emerging from the bathroom.

'Hi, Aunt Ruth. Mum, will you remind Jack that I'm waiting for an invitation to the farm?'

Ruth looked from Michael to her sister.

'I thought he was just your lawyer. Now I discover he's on first-name terms with your son!'

Libby ignored the remark and picked up her car keys.

'I'm going now. 'Night, Mike. Be good.'

She gave him a quick hug.

' 'Night, Mum.'

'Thanks, Ruth,' she said, opening the front door.

'Have fun,' Ruth called, smiling at her sister.

Libby closed the door behind her and took a deep breath. Fun? It was the last thing on her mind. She had never been so nervous. Why?

She was a grown woman, with a child and a mortgage, long past the stage of behaving like a schoolgirl.

Easing the car into first gear, she reflected it wouldn't be long before her sister was on the phone to their mother. Ruth couldn't help herself. Having decided her career was more important than marriage, she habitually made plans to marry off everyone else.

She should have told Ruth that Jack was nine years her junior. That would have shut her up. She smiled. Then again, maybe not. Knowing Ruth, she would have been investigating ways of meeting Jack herself! She was welcome to him.

She put Ruth out of her mind. What had the insurance company said, and why did Jack have to tell her over dinner? Why couldn't he just have called her into his office?

She pulled up in front of Jack's house. It stood as she remembered, old and sprawling, but kept in impeccable condition. The front door was open and light shone down the garden path. She passed through the gate as Jack came down the front steps. He wore a cotton shirt rolled up to his elbows, clean but faded jeans and he had bare feet. He looked relaxed, comfortable and happy.

They exchanged greetings and he led her back inside.

The Victorian house was beautifully preserved, with ornate cornices, stained-glass windows, and wooden floors. She caught sight of the living-room through an open door. The furniture was sumptuous and elegant, the floor scattered with rugs. Through another open door, she glimpsed a double bed and a velvet chaise-longue strewn with thick journals. Jack's room obviously.

'Oh, Jack, this is beautiful,' Libby breathed, entering the spacious kitchen.

Her eyes scanned the room, drinking in the high ceilings, the old kitchen dresser, slate floor and huge, walk-in pantry. A fragrant smell of tomatoes, onion and garlic hung in the air.

'Does your grandfather still live here?'

'No, I'm afraid he died shortly after you left the firm.'

'Oh, I'm so sorry. You must miss him terribly.'

'I do.'

He reached for an open bottle of wine and two glasses on the counter.

'Glass of red?' he asked gently.

'I'd love one. Do you live here alone?'

Was she being too inquisitive?

'Yes, but the house is too big for me. I'll have to sell it one of these days.'

'Oh, Jack, you mustn't do that! This is a house with character and memories, a house to be passed on to your children.'

'I don't have any children, yet.'

He handed her a glass of wine.

'I want to have children,' he went on, watching her face. 'Lots of them.'

'You do?'

She gripped her wine glass. For a second she had the odd sensation this topic had something to do with her!

'You haven't left yourself much time.'

'Don't worry, I'm working on it.'

He pushed the bottle to one side and raised his glass.

'To us,' he said.

To us? She supposed it was as good a toast as any.

He pulled out a bar stool.

'Have a seat while I finish off dinner.'

'What are you making? It smells delicious.'

'Just a tomato thing with seafood and pasta.'

Over the stove, he lifted a pot lid and stirred. Steam rose into the air. He forked out a piece of pasta and turned to her, blowing on it, holding it up to her mouth with his fingers.

'Is this done?'

There was no option but to open her mouth, let him feed her.

'Umm, I think so,' she spluttered, trying not to choke.

'We're ready to eat then.'

He piled a large, wooden tray with cutlery, serviettes, plates and an impressive-looking green salad.

'Don't tell me you made that, too,' she teased, brushing over the awkward moment.

Why had he fed her, touched his fingers to her mouth, and why did it matter so much? He laughed in response.

'No, I'm not much good at salads. I use the delicatessen around the corner, but I'm largely self-sufficient. I've been on my own for some time.'

She followed him on to a wooden deck and a table laid outside. She wanted to ask questions about his marriage, but that would be rude. He would tell her when he was ready.

'Are your parents still farming?' she asked, forking up some pasta.

'One of my brothers is managing Mum's and Dad's farm. He has his own adjoining property, so it's quite easy for him to keep an eye on them.'

He put down his fork and leaned back, tilting his chair against the wall.

'Which reminds me, I asked Michael if he would like to come to the farm. I understand he's never been to a farm.'

'He did mention it.'

She hesitated, feeling a twinge of guilt.

'I'm just not in the habit of letting him go off to places I don't know anything about.'

Jack could call her paranoid if he

liked but Michael was her child and her responsibility.

'I can understand that.'

His chair came forward suddenly with a thud, bringing his face within touching distance. His dark eyes gazed into hers. She drew back, alarmed.

'What's wrong?' He grinned. 'Frightened?'

She gave him a small smile and shook her head. It wasn't the noise of the chair that had startled her. It was the sudden proximity of his presence.

'You'll just have to come to the farm, too.'

'Oh, no, I couldn't do that!'

'Why not? My parents love having guests. There's plenty of room and Michael would have a whale of a time. Ashley, my brother, has two boys about his age, a third on the way.'

'It's very nice of you to ask, Jack, but, no, thank you.'

Michael would kill her if he knew she was turning Jack down. Why was she? And why did Jack want her to come?

She couldn't read the expression on his face. It was interested, but slightly bored, pressing, but careless. She reminded herself he was a criminal lawyer and steering her away from what he actually wanted was second nature to him. She picked up her empty plate and then put it down again. Where were her manners!

'Won't you tell me what the insurance company said, Jack?'

'So, that's what's bothering you. I'll put some coffee on.'

He began to load the tray.

'I'll use the bathroom while you're busy.'

She rose from her chair.

'It's down the passage, second on the left.'

She took out her lipstick in the bathroom and ran it over her lips. Why was Jack hedging over the letter? Was there something she didn't know? She ran a comb through her hair, stalling for time, telling herself there was nothing to be afraid of.

'Here, read it yourself.'

Jack stood in front of her back in the house and held out the letter. She dumped her coffee on a low table beside Jack's untouched mug and took the paper with trembling fingers, gazing up at Jack with apprehension. His face was grim.

'Read.'

She did as she was told, her eyes skimming over the words, faster and faster. The letter fell from her hands as she rose in a flurry.

'It's a lie, an out-and-out lie! They're trying to cover up something. They'll say anything!'

She walked across the room and back again, her chest tight. She felt she would explode. How dare they!

'Libby, I know it's hard for you, but there's an autopsy report verifying Simon's blood alcohol level attached to the letter. It appears genuine. I don't think I can dispute it.'

'But, Jack, Simon wasn't like that. He was lots of other things, but he never drank on the job.'

She turned to him, tears stinging her eyes.

'Are you sure? From what you've told me, he led a separate life.'

On the odd occasion, Simon might have had one too many, but with the lives of hundreds of people in his hands, never. It was absolutely unthinkable. She bent down and picked the letter up off the floor, re-read its blurred contents.

'Why didn't they produce this autopsy report at the hearing, Jack? Why drag it out now?'

'I don't know. Maybe they wanted to spare his family embarrassment.'

'It's a lie,' she reiterated, sniffing. 'I don't believe a word of it!'

The letter tight in her fist, she spun on her heel and began to pace the room again.

'Libby, calm down.'

She took a deep, shuddering breath. 'What?'

'Perhaps we can prove he wasn't

drunk if we can track down his movements before the flight took off.'

'What do you mean?'

'I mean find out who was with him. One of the flight crew must have known where he was, who was with him.'

'Jack, it'll be a woman and that sort of evidence will be all over the papers. You know I can't do that!'

He moved toward her.

'Why not? Isn't it more important to you to get your money?'

'No. There's Michael. I can't expose him to that. Imagine the other boys at school, the taunting that would go on.'

'Your son's very special to you, isn't he?'

She nodded.

'But what about you, and what Simon did to you?'

'You don't understand, Jack!'

He turned, his shoulders sagging visibly. For just a moment, she regretted being abrupt.

'So what are you going to do?' he asked.

'I don't know, but I'll think of something.'

She sat down heavily and picked up her coffee mug, but it wobbled so much she put it down again. Jack stood at the open french doors, silent.

'You don't believe me about Simon, do you?'

'I'm trying to, but they're offering me hard evidence and my instincts are telling me they're probably right.'

'Are you saying I'm lying, Jack?'

'No, of course not. I'm just saying you might not have the whole picture. There've been things you didn't know about Simon. Perhaps this is another one.'

She stood.

'I should go before we both say things we'll regret. Where's my handbag?'

She turned to leave the room, but stopped.

'You said instincts, Jack. Lawyers never trust their instincts, they only use hard proof. What proof do you have that you're not telling me about?'

'Oh, Libby, it's not connected with this!'

'What is it, Jack?'

'It's just something that happened years ago, not important.'

'Not important? Come on, Jack!'

He lowered his head and scuffed his foot on the rug as if he'd found something of vital importance in the carpet pile.

'Jack?'

'Simon behaved himself badly at an office Christmas party. He was drunk and he tried to do something unspeakable with one of the clerks.'

Jack raised his head and met her eyes. A flush warmed her neck and fanned into her cheeks. How could he? The office Christmas party of all places! Was there no end to Simon's indiscretions?

'Where was I?'

'From what I gathered, you were throwing up somewhere. You were pregnant at the time. Someone put you in a taxi and sent you home. I'm sorry, it slipped out. I never intended you to know.'

She hung her head, struck dumb by shame.

'Where are my things?' she managed to say at last.

'In the kitchen.'

Somehow she got out of the room. Fumbling for her handbag, her eyes blinded by tears, she suddenly under-stood the invitation to dinner, the need for the privacy of his home. He had only been thinking of her reaction, her feelings. When she returned from the kitchen, she put her head round the living-room door. Jack was slumped on the sofa, his head thrown back, his eyes closed. She softened her voice.

'Thank you for dinner. I can see myself out.'

He opened his eyes, but she didn't give him a chance to speak. She stumbled along the passage, down the garden path, blinking back her tears. She found her way to her car and got the door open, throwing her pashmina, handbag and the letter, still in her hand, across the front seat. She turned on the ignition, grinding the gears.

Barely seeing out of the windscreen, she wiped her eyes with the back of her hand, double de-clutched and tried first again. It went in smoothly and the vehicle pulled away from the kerb.

As she rounded the corner of Jack's street, she heard a scuffling noise. Before she could glance over her shoulder, something sharp and hard pressed into the back of her neck.

'Don't look round! Just keep going,' a man's voice said roughly.

Libby managed to keep going, somehow. She wanted to scream but she could hardly breathe. She ground the gears again and swore softly. She couldn't bring herself to glance in her rear-view mirror, but when she finally plucked up courage it was too dark to see anything other than an outline of a man's head.

'Easy now. You don't try anything, unless you want to feel this!'

He jerked the cold, hard implement so that its sharp edge grazed against her skin. She bit back a cry. The traffic light ahead was green. She slowed, hoping against hope it would turn red so she could stop. What she would do after that, she had no idea.

'I said, keep going, lady!'

She flinched, swinging out on to the main road. The man's breath at her shoulder was rough and coarse, like his accent.

'Turn left,' the voice said suddenly. 'Here!'

She screeched into a narrow side street, her hands jerking on the wheel like a learner driver.

'Here! Stop! You stop!'

Reflexes obedient, her foot jammed on the brake pedal. The car lurched forwards, and the sharp implement dug into the back of her neck. Involuntarily she cried out and put up her arm. It was caught and cruelly held by a gloved hand. Her skin crawled.

'You try something, lady, and you get

hurt! Now you tell that lawyer, you listening to me?'

She nodded.

'You tell him to stay away from Waterson Constructions. This is a warning. Next time . . . '

He left the suggestion hanging in the air. She nodded again.

'Tell me what I said!'

Libby repeated it woodenly, her tongue thick in her mouth, her heart pressed up against her throat.

'Good,' he said, 'you get the message. Now I get out here. Don't look.'

The door opened and she heard movement behind her, the door slamming. He tapped on her window. She opened it marginally, her eyes looking straight ahead. She didn't want to see the face, the face that must match the ugly voice.

'Next time, you know what will happen,' he said, menace in his tone.

'What'll happen?'

He chuckled, a sound with no amusement in it.

84

'I know and he will find out.'

A full minute passed before she realised he had actually gone. She didn't look back as she shot the car forward, taking the corner too fast, the vehicle swaying drunkenly over the road. She slowed at the next junction, but didn't stop. The shadows at the side of the road had a life of their own. She sped off, exceeding the speed limit, praying she would meet a policeman.

Ruth was asleep on the couch when she got through the door. Libby told her journalist sister nothing. She saw her to her car, making all the right responses. Yes, she'd had a good evening, and, no, there hadn't been any funny business, as Ruth put it.

She waved goodbye, then sprinted back to the house as soon as Ruth pulled away, locking the door behind her. She looked in on Michael and covered him with the quilt. Then, taking the dog with her, she forced herself to go through every room, checking behind the doors and under the beds.

Childhood superstitions died hard.

She was making herself a cup of tea in the kitchen when the phone rang. Her heart thudded against her ribs. Who would be ringing at this hour of night? Did the man know where she lived? She picked up the receiver and said hello. She was gravel-voiced, like someone had their hands around her throat.

'Libby? I'm sorry about tonight. I didn't mean to upset you.'

'Oh, Jack.'

Her voice quavered. A big lump formed in her throat, making breathing difficult, talk almost impossible. She had to let it all out.

'There was a man . . . '

'A man? Where?'

She couldn't answer.

'Libby? What's the matter? What's happened?' Jack became agitated. 'Say something, damn it!'

'I'll be all right, in a minute.'

The tears ran freely down her cheeks. She took a deep breath.

'There was a man in my car.'

'What? I'll be there as soon as I can. Don't open the door to anyone,' he said harshly.

'That's not necessary,' she began, but he had hung up.

She didn't want him to come round, but, at the same time, she was relieved he was coming. A man in the room, especially a man as big as Jack, would make her feel safe. She went into the living-room. Turning the light off, she pulled the curtain slightly open, and waited in the darkness.

The letter from the insurance company came back to her. She'd hardly had time to absorb the information, let alone think constructively about it. She had no doubt they were covering up, but why? There was no question of searching for Simon's companion. She didn't want Michael to be exposed to anything more. The child had been through enough. She would rather they were poor and happy, than rich and traumatised. She'd been poor before, it was nothing new.

And now this — Jack in danger! He'd hinted as much. What if something happened to him? Her eyes filled with tears again. She couldn't bear to think about consequences, about things happening to him.

A vehicle motored slowly down her street, and a sports car drew up outside her gate. Under the street light, the tall frame of Jack emerged from the car.

'I told you not to open the door,' he said sternly when she let him in.

'But I knew it was you,' she said, locking the door behind her.

She eyed the suit, briefcase and holdall he carried.

'It looks like you've come to stay for a week.'

'I have.'

He dropped everything on to the hall carpet where he stood.

'Now what happened?'

'Jack, there's absolutely no need for you to stay! I'm quite all right.'

'I didn't come here to argue.'

'People will talk.'

'People talk anyway.'

'What about Michael?'

'What about Michael? We'll be in separate rooms. I can't see there's a problem. As I see it, you might just be glad of my company. Now, will you please tell me what happened?'

He stood, crowding the passage, staring at her. A slate blue jumper had been thrown over his shirt and he'd pulled on a pair of runners. In answer, she swept her hair off her neck and backed up to him.

'I can't see my neck. What's the damage?'

Strong, gentle hands touched her skin.

'He did this to you?'

She nodded.

'He didn't hurt you anywhere else?'

'No.'

'Was this the same man who jumped me?' he asked sharply.

'I don't know. I didn't see his face. All I know is he's foreign, as his English is broken. He could be Asian or he could be European. He was only in the car for a few minutes. He got out down the road.'

She felt something light and soft touch the back of her neck.

'What're you doing?' she asked sharply.

'Kissing it better. Where's that antiseptic you doused me with so liberally?'

'In the bathroom cupboard.'

He padded down the passage. The light switch clicked and the bathroom cupboard squeaked. He knew his way around her house! Why did that fact alarm her? She was becoming too familiar with him, that's why. She was, after all, older than he was. She shouldn't let herself forget that.

'Come on,' he said, 'into the kitchen.'

'I have to give you a message,' she said, gritting her teeth.

He was patting the graze with cottonwool soaked in antiseptic. It stung like billyho. She turned, watched him replace the lid of the bottle.

'He said I must tell you to stay away from Waterson Constructions, that this was just a warning. Next time . . . '

She couldn't finish the sentence.

'Blast,' Jack said softly, following that up with a few choice expletives. 'Sorry,' he muttered, catching her eye.

He pushed himself away from the counter.

'Just as well I brought all my gear. Is that bed in the spare room still made up?'

'Jack, you're not staying.'

He took her wrists, stilling her argument. He looked tired, more tired than she felt, and worried.

'Libby, listen carefully. I lied to you the other night.'

Her mouth fell open.

'I know I should never lie, particularly not to you, but I was trying to protect you. I didn't want to alarm you. That man who assaulted me, I think he's involved in Waterson's somehow. He's seen you with me, and he thinks he can get at me by hurting you. I can't prove a thing, yet. You're in this situation because of me. The least I can do is offer some sort of protection. You may not think you need me but what about Michael? His life may be in danger, too. You won't argue with that, will you?'

Libby opened her mouth to speak but no words came. If anything happened to Michael she would die.

'In the morning, I'll organise a private detective. I don't want this to go any further.'

'Is it that serious?'

'Yes. You really don't remember what the bloke looked like?'

She pulled a hand out of his grasp and made a gesture in the air.

'I told you, I couldn't see his face. I had a screw driver stuck in the back of my neck!'

'I'm sorry. I'm forgetting you must have been terribly frightened.'

He let go of her wrist and pulled her into his arms. She let him hold her, feeling the warmth of his body, the comfort of another human being.

'Mum?'

Michael stood in the doorway. She pulled away from Jack.

'Hello, sweetheart.'

'Can I have a drink of water?' Michael mumbled, ignoring Jack.

Libby found a glass and poured him some water. When he was finished, she put her arm around his shoulder and led him back to bed.

'Who's that in the kitchen?' he asked, sleepily.

'It's Jack. He's going to sleep in the spare room.'

'Jack!'

He was instantly awake.

'Can I ask him about the farm?'

'No! Not now, Mikie. In the morning. Go to sleep now.'

She kissed him briefly on the forehead, wishing that life was as uncomplicated as he saw it. Down the passage, someone had turned on the light in the spare bedroom. She found

93

Jack hanging up his suit on the wardrobe door.

'I hope my being here hasn't caused any problems.'

'No, but I still don't think it's necessary.'

Avoiding her assertion, he dumped his holdall from the bed to the floor and came to the door.

' 'Night, Libby,' he said, gently running a finger down her cheek.

' 'Night, Jack.'

She turned away quickly, his touch sending shivers down her spine.

There was an explanation, she told herself firmly, she was emotionally distressed.

In the morning, she went down the passage and woke Michael. The door to Jack's room was open but he wasn't in it, and the bed was made up. She found him in the kitchen with the kettle on, looking in her cupboards.

'Right hand cupboard, below the kettle.'

'Thank you,' he said, pulling out two

mugs. 'How are you this morning? Sleep well? Tea or coffee?'

She clutched the lapels of her dressing-gown tighter across her chest and blinked.

'What? Jack, I'm not a morning person. One question at a time.'

'Not a morning person? What a shame. Tea or coffee?'

'Tea, please. Strong, one sugar. Have you finished in the bathroom?'

'Yes, only I seem to have forgotten my socks. You wouldn't happen to have a spare pair, would you?'

'I'll see what I can do.'

Thoroughly awake, Libby departed, clutching her tea.

The sight of Jack, immaculate in a crisp white shirt and tailored trousers, his short dark hair still wet from the shower, had sharpened her wits. There were another three mornings to face before the weekend, another three mornings of Jack in her kitchen!

* * *

95

'Libby, this is Nigel Murdoch, the private detective I've hired.'

Jack's eyes met hers briefly at the door that evening as she traipsed in with Michael and the dog. She'd given Jack his own key, so he could come and go as he wished.

'Hello,' Libby said as Murdoch enveloped her hand warmly.

He was pleasant looking with a moustache and kind eyes and built like a prop forward. Early thirties, she surmised.

'This is my son, Michael.'

She put her arm around Mike's shoulders.

'I'll be back in a minute.'

She went down the hallway with Michael, settled him in the kitchen with his homework and let out the dog. She rejoined the two men in the livingroom as they were discussing fees.

'Twenty-four hour surveillance will cost you,' Murdoch said, 'after yourself and the other two.'

'I don't think we need to worry about

surveillance for me.'

Murdoch raised his eyebrows.

'It's your call, but given the circumstances I would recommend it.'

Jack shook his head, dismissing the idea. Murdoch turned to Libby.

'Libby, do you mind running over last night's events with me? Jack's told me all he knows, I just need your input.'

The private detective's enquiring eyes met hers. She told him what had happened, trying not to leave anything out and giving him an impression of the man who had attacked Jack as well. At last he closed his notebook.

'That's it then, I'll be off.'

As he stood, Libby saw Murdoch take in the row of family photos on the bookshelf. There was one of Simon, looking very handsome in his uniform. Strange how she could look at Simon without feeling anything.

Jack locked the door behind Murdoch.

'That's done, I feel much better, don't you? What are we having for dinner? I'm starving. If you like I could get some Chinese food.'

'Thanks, but I've already organised the beginnings of a stir-fry. How was your day?'

'Typically busy, but I've brought no work home. I might even have that game of chess with Mike.'

'Perhaps you can check his homework while I start the dinner.'

'Sure thing,' he said, and he put his arm comfortingly around her shoulder as they went down the passage.

'Where did you find Murdoch? He seems rather nice,' she asked.

'He's an old school friend, an ex-rugby player.'

Dinner was soon over and Michael in bed more or less on time. She left his bedroom door ajar as she went to see how Jack was getting on in the kitchen. He had insisted on clearing up. Whistling to himself, he ran clean water through the sink and wiped down the draining-board.

'Very domesticated.'

She leaned against the doorjamb, watching him.

'I can thank my grandfather for that,' he replied. 'I'll even do some ironing if you like!'

'You mean you really haven't brought any work home?'

'No, not tonight. I'm all yours.'

He took the tea towel and hung it up. Tucking his hands into his pockets, he stood and looked at her.

What was she going to do with him?

'Perhaps we could play backgammon, unless you want to watch TV?'

He pulled out a bar stool and sat down.

'I don't watch the box, except when I'm very tired and I haven't played backgammon for years. I might have to do some cheating.'

'I don't think it's possible to cheat at backgammon,' she said, rummaging in a cupboard for the set. 'And I didn't think you cheated at anything.'

She trailed off, thinking of Simon who had cheated often and well, and not just at backgammon.

'Unlike some other man you knew?'

She focused her attention on setting up the game.

'You seem to know what I'm thinking more often than not. How do you do it?'

'Co-incidence.'

'Did your ex-wife cheat on you?'

The question came out of the blue. Libby was horrified. She had told herself she wasn't going to pry into his life.

'I never cared to find out.'

'So, what did she do?'

He fiddled with the counters, saying nothing.

'Or was it something you did?' she encouraged gently.

'I shouldn't have married her, that's all. I wasn't in love with her. She wasn't in love with me, either. She was in love with the idea of being married.'

He picked up the dice, rattled them in his hand, avoiding her eyes.

'You weren't in love with her and you

married her? How could you?'

He raised his face to hers at last. His eyes were bright as if he was having trouble keeping his emotions in check.

'I'd had a bad experience. I'd been in love with a married woman, a relationship that was going nowhere. I know that's no excuse, but I was on the rebound.'

He threw the dice down on the table.

'Oh, look, I've thrown a six,' he crowed. 'Can we start?'

5

She woke in the morning with Jack bending over her bed. She stared up at him in alarm.

'What is it?' she asked. 'What are you doing in my bedroom?'

'It's time to get ready for work. I've brought you some tea, strong, the way you like it. Don't go back to sleep. You've only got half-an-hour.'

'You let me sleep in on purpose, didn't you?' she accused, noticing he was having trouble keeping a straight face.

'I've got some points to catch up on,' he said, ducking out the door.

'Have you decided what you're going to do about the letter from the insurance company?' he asked her later in the car.

'I think so.'

'And?'

'And nothing. I haven't made a decision to put it on paper.'

'Don't leave it too late. If you procrastinate, they'll think they've got you where they want you.'

'Yes, Jack.'

She closed her eyes. Why did he have to spoil the morning by bringing that up? But he was right, it was important.

'If you want my advice, I'm happy to talk,' he persisted.

'I know you are, thanks. But it's something I have to decide on my own.'

'As you like, just don't leave it too late.'

He swung the car into a parking place marked Williams & Nash and switched off the ignition. Leaning in towards her, he fumbled for something on the passenger side floor. She stiffened, her eyes inches from his head. She could just make out his head wound. It looked like the stitches had been removed. As if aware of her scrutiny, Jack turned his head.

'I'd like to get this business over as much as you would, Libby.'

Gripping an umbrella, he drew back and straightened in his seat.

'It's hanging over you and it's hanging over me, over us. I can't get anything done.'

'If it's taking up too much of your time, I'm sorry.'

'That's not what I meant. You know what I mean.'

'I do?'

Libby frowned. What was he talking about?

'I'm going to be caught up in court for the next couple of days with the Waterson case,' he went on. 'You won't see a lot of me. Please, don't do anything silly.'

He turned her face and kissed her tenderly on the forehead. She had a close-up of a strong, freshly-shaven jaw above a pristine white shirt, the smell of soap and water. Fumbling for the handle, she opened the car door and got out in a hurry.

'Thanks for the lift. I'll get the train home.'

He shot out of the car.

'I don't want you to get the train home. It isn't safe. I want you to take my car. I'll get a taxi.'

In the days that followed, she didn't see much of Jack, but she found his breakfast bowl rinsed and packed into the dishwasher every morning. She discovered his shirts in the laundry basket with a note. If she would be kind enough to put them through the wash, he would iron them. Naturally she ironed them and left them hanging in his room. It felt strange and yet comforting at the same time.

On Sunday, his bedroom door was closed. A note taped to the door read, *Please leave me to sleep*. She and Michael went to lunch with her parents and when they returned Jack was gone again.

One night she came home with Michael and found the private detective, Murdoch, on his beat, hanging around her front gate. She'd been conscious of his presence, but it was the first time he'd shown his face. They exchanged greetings, and as people will, talked about the weather, Murdoch remarking on the autumn chill in the air.

'Wouldn't you like to come in for a hot coffee?' Libby offered.

'I'd love a coffee,' he told her, 'but I can't come in.'

'Not a problem. I'll bring us a mug out here.'

She busied herself in the kitchen while Michael fed the dog and started his homework. It seemed strange — inside, domesticity and outside, a detective guarding them. Libby took out the coffee.

'Have you known Jack long?' she asked.

'I went to school with him. We're old mates.' He sipped at his coffee, then he said, 'I saw your husband.'

Puzzled, Libby drew her eyebrows together.

'You mean the photograph on the shelf in the house?'

It was a good likeness of Simon, but why was he bringing it up?

'No, not the photograph. I saw your husband the night before the accident.'

He paused, waiting for her to understand.

'You mean before the crash? Before . . . '

Her brain was trying to work.

'Yes, that's right, before the flight. I met him in a bar.'

'You knew him?'

'I didn't say that. It was a coincidence. I was in the town on business, staying at the same hotel where the aircrew was based. I had a drink before dinner at the bar. He was sitting on a stool alongside me and we started chatting.'

'Was he drinking?'

'Oh, yes, he was drinking all right.'

He paused, looked at her, watching her face. She held her breath.

'He was drinking orange juice. I wanted to buy him a drink, but he said he never drank the night before a flight.'

The air came out of her lungs with a great shudder. Her coffee mug wobbled noticeably.

'Why are you telling me this?'

Murdoch placed his coffee mug on the step and clasped his hands over his knees. He looked satisfied.

'I wanted to see your reaction. It was a long shot.'

'My reaction? What are you saying?'

'Let's just say I'm doing some work for a client.'

Libby frowned.

'I'm not following you at all.'

'You're not meant to be.'

She stiffened.

'You can't say things like that and then not explain them.'

'I shouldn't have said anything at all. I was out of order.' He paused a moment, then said, 'I'm investigating your insurance company.'

'My insurance company?'

She kept repeating everything he said!

'How would you know about my insurance company?'

Murdoch's moustache bristled.

'I'm trained to see things other people don't. I saw an envelope lying on your coffee table with the insurance company's address in one corner, your name on the front. Then I saw the photograph of you husband on the shelf. Of course, I knew about your husband having been killed. There was such a fuss in the papers at the time. I decided your husband must have been insured with the same company. Why else would you have a letter from them lying around? If it was any other kind of letter you would have filed it, but this one you left out. Perhaps its contents worry you. Perhaps you still need to reply to it? I made some deductions, asked myself why you had left the letter out on the coffee table, why its contents worry you. Now I've asked you some leading questions and got the reaction I was looking for. All very simple, really.'

'Are you saying you're investigating the insurance company for fraudulence?'

'I'm not saying anything. In fact I will deny anything I've said to you here tonight. I need more time and more facts. Will you tell me what you know, about the insurance company, what they've said to you?'

Libby told him and he absorbed the information thoughtfully.

'Can I bring you out some dinner?' she asked after a while.

He smiled.

'Thank you, but no. I must return to my work, to my beat. Your safety is my job.'

He rose, held out his hand and she took it.

'I'll be in touch. Thank you for the coffee and for everything else.'

'Oh, no, it's I who must thank you,' she insisted.

★   ★   ★

Jack came into her office early one morning, a week after she'd last seen him. He looked haggard. Dark rings circled his eyes. She knew the case must be taking it out of him; she was following it in the papers.

'Did you know there's a long weekend coming up?'

She nodded.

'I'm going to the farm. I need some rest. I want you and Michael to come with me.'

'Jack, there's no need.'

He checked his watch.

'I don't have a lot of time to argue with you. I'm meant to be over at court right now. I'm not leaving you in town. Either you come with me, or I stay in town and, if it's all the same to you, I'd really like to get away.'

She narrowed her gaze.

'Are you blackmailing me, Jack Trennery?'

He raised a smile, relief evident in his eyes.

'Pack casual clothes. We'll do some

horseriding. I want to leave straight from the office on Friday evening. Ask Murdoch if he can bring Michael in after school and meet us here,' he added.

'I haven't said yes.'

'You will.'

He moved towards her desk, leaned in towards her.

'Give me a kiss for luck.'

'Oh, Jack,' she said in exasperation.

But she leaned forward and touched her mouth to his cheek. Withdrawing her face, she met his eyes. He opened his mouth, began to say something, then shut it again.

'Be careful,' she said, then he was gone.

At home, she did some quick packing for the weekend, jeans and shirts, a dress, just in case, and a change of clothes for Michael, too. Jack probably had clothes at the farm. When you went there as regularly as every weekend, you didn't want to be bothered with baggage. No doubt, you had a bed made up for you with pyjamas under the pillow.

She then rang her mother.

'Who is this man you're going out with?' her mother asked.

'I'm not going out with him, Mum, I work with him, that's all. He's a lawyer from the office. He seems to have taken a shine to Michael, invited him to his farm for the weekend and I'm tagging along. I'm sorry we won't be able to come down and see you.'

There was no need to tell her anything else.

'You'll have to bring him round to meet us.'

'Mum, it's not like that! He's years younger than I am. He's just a friend.'

'All the same, we'd like to meet him,' she persisted.

'How's Dad?'

In desperation, Libby changed the subject.

'Oh, you know, his usual self. Got a bee in his bonnet about the golf club now. He says they're conspiring to get him off the committee.'

'They probably are,' Libby retorted.

She adored her father, but she knew he could be difficult. The chit-chat went on pleasantly. After a while, Libby rang off, promising she would catch up with them both soon.

The farm was an hour's drive from Melbourne and it was dark by the time they reached the white pillars at the entrance to the homestead. Jack's parents, Fran and Tom, came out of the house to welcome them. Jack had Fran's dark eyes but Tom's height.

Fran made a pot of tea and produced a fruit cake, and they sat in the kitchen, Jack prowling the room because he said he needed to stretch his legs. It wasn't long before the older couple excused themselves for bed. Jack helped Libby clear away the tea things, then he led Michael and her out to the guest quarters.

The two comfortably-furnished rooms each contained a set of twin beds with pretty floral curtains and an en-suite bathroom they shared. Libby riffled through a holdall and produced Michael's pyjamas and toothbrush. She put them into his hand and pushed him wordlessly in the direction of the bathroom.

Jack went across to a bed and sat down. Then he got up and went across to the open doorway, looking out. Why didn't he say good-night and leave? He must be exhausted. She touched him gently on the arm.

'See you in the morning, Jack.'

He turned.

'Is Michael in bed yet?'

'Almost.'

'Go and say good-night to him. There's something I want to show you.'

Outside, the night air was crisp, with a cloudless sky and a waxing moon. Jack took her hand.

'It's dark until you get accustomed to it,' he explained.

Libby followed his dim outline. He led her away from the house along a worn track that climbed upwards through the scrub. When they came out on top of a hillock, he stopped. Puffing a little, she inhaled the clean, cold air. It smelled very different to the city air she knew. Below, she could make out the lights of the homestead flickering within a semi-circle of trees.

In the darkness Jack waved an arm down towards the right.

'That rundown, ramshackle building you probably can't see over in the distance is mine. I've had it for some time, but I'm planning to pull it down and build a new homestead.'

With his other hand he held on to her firmly. It was a long time since anyone had held her hand and she was content to let it be.

'What do you think? You're not saying much,' he commented.

'I'm speechless. It's all so . . . so . . . the night, the stars . . . darkness. I'd forgotten what it's like out in the country. Beautiful's not really the word. I can't find the word.'

'Libby,' he said gently, 'I'm going to

rebuild the homestead because I've found someone to share it with.'

Stunned, she took a breath.

'You have?' she swallowed, feeling a ridiculous twinge of jealousy.

Who was this mysterious woman and why hadn't Jack mentioned her before? She swallowed.

'Oh, Jack, I'm so happy for you. Is it someone I know?'

'It's you. I love you, Libby. I always have. I know this is soon, 'way too soon, no doubt, but I can't wait any longer to tell you. Will you marry me?'

Marry him? She struggled with the concept of what he was saying. He couldn't mean her, surely? There must be some mistake. She went over his words in her mind, opened her mouth to speak, to object, but no sound emerged.

'Libby?'

'Jack, don't be silly. It's ridiculous. Marry you?'

Words tumbled out of her mouth, not very sensible, but words nonetheless.

Then she laughed, a brittle sound in the frosty night air, not a laugh of happiness at all.

'You can't mean me! Is this one of your jokes? If it is, I'm not amused.'

He put his arms around her, drew her gently against him. She smelled again the fresh, clean masculine smell that was Jack, then struggled out of his embrace.

'This is not a joke,' he said.

'Jack, you seem to have forgotten something. I'm older than you. You're just a boy.'

'I am not a boy!' he exploded.

He was still gripping her hand. He reeled her in against him and she went, mesmerised by the shine of his dark eyes. It was a long, slow and seductive kiss that followed. Her blood pounding in her ears, she turned. She had to get away! She picked her way over the rough terrain and grasses, trying to find the path, trying to escape.

Someone caught her hand, held her fast. He had come after her.

'Is that the only reason you're turning me down, because I'm younger than you?'

'No — I mean, yes, I mean — '

'Which is it, Libby?'

She took a quavering breath. How could he do this to her? They were friends. Now he had wrecked it all!

'I thought you were my friend, Jack.'

'I am your friend! I just happen to love you, too. I've been loving you for years. Remember I told you I'd been in love with a married woman, a relationship that was going nowhere? Libby, that woman was you!'

He paused, softened his voice.

'By some miracle, you've walked back into my life. I'm not going to let you go a second time.'

'Oh, Jack, I can't marry you.'

'Why is the age difference worrying you? Plenty of men marry older women. It's worked for them, why shouldn't it work for us? And anyway, if you love someone you can do anything.'

He came to a halt. The sound of his

breathing, quickened by his tirade, filled her ears.

'I don't love you, Jack.'

His mouth opened, then closed again. He went very still.

'Why are you crying, then?' he asked at last.

'Crying?'

She put her hand up to her face. It was wet with tears. She took a hurried step backwards, and another. Half-sobbing, she turned and stumbled wildly down the track. Somehow she found the door of the guest cottage, pushed it open, closed it, shot the bolt, and leaned heavily against it.

How could she marry Jack? She was nine years older than him. Nine years! She would lose her looks long before he did. He would tire of her. She would be a millstone around his neck. She would go through the same heartache she had with Simon. Jack would divorce her or, worse still, have affairs. Her breath caught in her throat, choked her. The thought of Jack having an affair was almost more than she could bear. And that was all assuming she loved him!

'Are you there, Libby?'

He was at the door. She couldn't see him but she could feel his presence, intense, alive.

'I know you're there,' he said, his voice muffled by the wood. 'Open the door, please. Let me talk to you.'

She held her breath.

'You love me, I know you do.'

Her breath came out in a rush. She pushed herself away from the door, lurched towards the bathroom. The edge of the bath was cool. In the dark she perched on it and put her face in her hands.

'I don't love you, Jack, I don't love you, Jack,' she intoned, blocking out everything else.

She stopped suddenly, her eyes overflowing with tears.

If she didn't love Jack, why was she so afraid to open the door?

6

At breakfast next morning Jack acted as if the events of the preceding night had never taken place. More than likely, Libby mused, he had come to his senses. No doubt he now wanted to forget the whole episode.

Buttering her toast, she decided to take Jack's lead, pretend it was all a bad dream. She let her mind drift away from Jack, watching his mother stir her coffee.

Two cups of coffee later, Ashley arrived with his two boys. There were horses to be ridden and streams to be fished, and within minutes Michael was bantering with his new friends.

With their departure to the nearest stream, the breakfast dishes were washed and dried, and Fran and Tom were soon occupied doing chores. There was nowhere to run. Jack, his eyes catching Libby unawares, suggested a walk over to the stables.

Stammering a little, she agreed, telling herself she must behave normally. After all she was a grown-up and Jack was not a boy. That had been the wrong thing to say. He was a man, a man who knew how to kiss. Just thinking about it made her knees feel weak. How could she have thought him otherwise, she thought as he led her into the stable.

'I thought you said you could ride!'

Libby tried not to let her fear show as with white knuckles, she clung to the reins as the horse moved beneath her.

'Well, I lied, didn't I?'

'You? Tell lies?'

Jack clicked his tongue on the roof of his mouth in mock disbelief.

'Why do you have to be so right, so often, Jack! Isn't there anything I can do better than you?'

He looked searchingly at her from behind the horse's muzzle where he was fiddling with bits of leather.

'I didn't realise it mattered so much to you.'

It didn't. Why was she losing her sense of humour? She should never have agreed to this ride! He moved to her side and rested his hand on the saddle, threw himself across the back of the horse, and sat up behind her.

'Besides,' he continued in her ear, 'there are plenty of things you can do better than me.'

Were there? She wasn't sure what they were, but she wasn't going to ask. He settled himself into the saddle, put one hand around her waist and pulled her up hard against his body.

'Comfortable?' he asked.

Jammed up against his chest, his breath in her hair, his long thighs touching hers — how could anyone be comfortable?

Taking the reins, he dug his knees into the stallion's sides and turned the horse towards the stable door. The view outside took her mind off Jack. The countryside lay before them, the land dry and brown. Mobs of sheep scattered themselves out on the paddocks. It was a glorious day. Clouds drifted across the deep blue sky and the air smelled fresh and good.

'What a view. I bet you never tire of looking at this.'

Jack hesitated.

'The old homestead I showed you last night looks worse in the daytime, doesn't it?'

Libby stiffened. Why had he brought up last night? She didn't want to think about last night.

'It's really time I did something about it,' he went on.

'How long have you owned it?' she asked tentatively, although she really didn't want to talk about it, but she couldn't appear to be rude.

'I bought it some time ago to increase the size of our combined properties. My family uses the land, but the house . . . '

He shrugged.

'You've never lived in it?'

'It's not habitable in its present state, and it's built far too close to the main road. There, do you see that strip of dirt running along behind it where the dust is rising? That's the main farm road. I don't know who's on it,' he said in puzzlement, seeing dust rising. 'We're not expecting anybody.'

The horse turned abruptly and headed downhill. Libby gave a little gasp and pushed back against Jack.

'Hey, it's OK,' he reassured her. 'It's just a little slope. Would you like to wait here? I have to go and see who it is. We've had squatters before.'

She averted her eyes and focused on the distant, rundown farmstead.

'I'll be fine,' she said, swallowing.

Once the land levelled off, Jack urged the horse forward. Libby wished the ground were not so far away. She wished she'd stayed at the farmhouse with Fran and baked scones.

The roof of the cottage, she soon saw, was falling in, and birds had made nests in the eaves. Most of the window panes were missing or had been smashed. They circled the building and there they saw the vehicle, carefully hidden from view, parked between the dwelling and what had once been the stables. Jack swung himself off the horse and gave her the reins.

'I'm going in to check. Stay here. I won't be long.'

He turned on his heel and strode towards the back entrance of the house.

'Jack?'

All at once, she was concerned. He swung around impatiently.

'Don't do anything I wouldn't do.'

Jack made scoffing noises. He thrust his hands into his pockets and disappeared through the gloom of the doorway. The horse immediately began to fidget. It flicked its tail clear across Libby's leg, and she nearly fell off in fright, and still the farmhouse remained quiet. What was he doing?

If only she knew how to get off the horse! Every time she contemplated climbing off, the animal somehow sensed it and side-stepped. She could see herself sprawled in the dust, one foot caught in the stirrup.

Suddenly a shout echoed from the cottage. The stallion's ears went back, his neck stiffening. Something heavy hit the ground, followed almost immediately by sounds of thrashing and thumping. Then a gun went off, and the horse reared.

Any thoughts for Jack's safety were overridden by the necessity to stay in the saddle. She clung to whatever she could lay her hands on, reins, mane, neck. Her breath came in gasps each time the stallion's front legs hit the ground, her thigh muscles ached with the effort of remaining upright.

Breaking into a canter, the horse headed back the way they had come. Libby pulled hard on the reins, trying to stop the beast. How could they go home without Jack? It changed direction suddenly, veering back and returning to the building. She pulled on the reins again and it came to a halt, its hooves stamping the ground with impatience.

'Here, boy, here, boy,' she said soothingly, her own breath coming in great gulps of nervousness.

Movement near the door caught her eye, and a swarthy, stocky man emerged from the gloom, mouthing words at her. He had a gun gripped at his side. He raised it and pointed it at her. He shouted and gesticulated with his free arm. Instinctively, she shielded her face, cried out, but no sound disturbed the air. He didn't shout. The horse fidgeted. Cautiously, she lowered her hand, concentrated on what he was saying.

'Get out of here! You tell anybody, I kill him. You understand?'

He spat into the ground, lowering the weapon. Something moved in the dark doorway and Jack stumbled out into the light. His shirt was torn and dirty and blood trickled down the side of his face, dripping on to his collar. His head wound had been reopened.

'Jack!' she cried out in anguish.

Her voice broke and turned the sound of his name into a wail. The man pointed the weapon at her again and swore.

'No!'

Jack flung himself at his assailant, but whatever had happened in the cottage had dulled his reflexes. The man threw out an arm and the gun caught Jack across the face. Reeling backwards he staggered against the doorframe, sliding down to a heap on the ground.

Libby strangled a scream.

The man trained the gun back on to her. He scowled, jerked his head.

'Go now! You go!'

'Go,' she repeated inanely to the horse, 'go.'

The horse didn't move. Her eyes flew back to the man who took a step towards her. She stayed calm, remembering to press her knees in against the horse's sides as she had seen Jack do.

It worked. The horse trotted forward. She pressed harder. The horse cantered.

She closed her eyes with grim relief. She breathed in little bursts, expecting at any second to slip and fall. Moments later, she was still in the saddle. She glanced back over her shoulder. The man was gone and Jack no longer slumped in a heap in the doorway.

She patted the horse on the side of the neck. He was heading in the right direction.

'Good boy,' she said, unable to remember his name.

She had to find Jack's brother. She hoped Ashley was level-headed. From what little she had seen of him this morning when he'd come by with his two boys, he appeared to be. Thoughts flew through her head. They must get the police, but Ashley first. What should she tell Jack's parents? Ashley would decide that. He would decide how much they needed to know.

The image of Jack in the doorway, bleeding and subdued, kept reappearing before her eyes. He had risked his life by throwing himself at the gunman, all for her. He could have been killed.

The stablehand was in the yard, pitchfork in hand, when she reached the paddock.

'Jack's been hurt,' she said as he helped her dismount. 'I need transport quickly. Please don't tell anyone until I've spoken to Ashley.'

He pushed his hat back and raised his eyebrows.

'Truck's over there, ma'am, help yourself.'

She got in, and found the keys in the ignition. She took off slowly down the road, catching sight of Jack's mother setting off to the henhouse. Forcing herself, she waved and smiled.

There was no sign of anybody around at Ashley's. Making her way to the homestead's back door, she could hear movement in the kitchen. Libby knew Ashley's wife, Claire, was eight months pregnant. She had hoped to avoid her, not wanting to put her under any unnecessary stress.

'Hi, Claire,' she said casually at the back door.

It took a supreme effort to keep her voice calm. Through the flyscreen, she could see the other woman at the kitchen table folding washing. Claire looked up at Libby, mouth open in surprise.

'I'm Libby, Michael's mum. It's so nice of you to have him. Do you know where Ashley is? Jack sent me to get him. There's a fence Jack would like him to look at.'

'Oh, hello,' Claire said. 'Nice to meet you. The boys are over at the stables. Ashley's in the shed.'

'Where's Mick, the stablehand?' a male voice asked behind her. 'He usually helps Jack. I don't get involved when Jack's around.'

Libby turned. Ashley was not quite as tall as Jack, but more powerfully built, and just as good-looking.

'He's caught up with other things. This is really urgent.'

With her back to Claire, she gave

Ashley a slow wink and jerked her head. The moment wasn't lost on Jack's brother. He narrowed his eyes. The vision of Jack as she had last seen him swam before her eyes again and her lower jaw wobbled.

'See you later, Claire,' she said unevenly.

She set off for the truck. Claire said something and Ashley murmured a reply. The screen door banged and a moment later he was at her side.

'What's up?'

'Get in,' she said as they reached the truck.

She started the ignition. He sat bunched up against the passenger door, staring at her.

'Has this happened before?' he asked when she had poured out the whole story.

'Nothing this bad. He's been assaulted and he's had threats on his life. He says it's all to do with his case.'

Ashley swore softly.

'Why hasn't he said anything?'

'He's a very private person. You must know that,' she said as they drew closer to his parents' homestead.

'Perhaps this man never intended to take Jack. Perhaps you surprised him and having Jack walk in like that was too good an opportunity to miss.'

She turned off the ignition. They could see Tom Trennery in the woolshed. Ashley swung open his door.

'Come on, let's go tell the old man.'

'Aren't you going to call the police?'

'No.'

'No? Why not?'

He bent down and peered at her through the open door.

'If we get the police involved, it'll be tomorrow before we get Jack out of there. He may be dead by then.'

'But — '

'Trust me,' he said, closing the door.

Libby put her hand tiredly up to her forehead. Her stomach felt empty, and she was cold. She must be in shock. Jack's face kept reappearing before her eyes. After a minute, she made a determined effort and got out of the car.

Tom Trennery saw her coming.

'The first thing you need is a cup of sweet tea, my girl,' he said later, taking her arm.

'Tea? There's no time for tea.'

'You're as white as a sheet.'

'I am?'

'Let me do the talking to Fran,' Tom said confidently, leading her into the homestead. 'We're going to need her help.'

'You have a plan?'

'Yes,' Ashley said beside her. 'Dad'll tell you. I'm going back now. I'll be over about six. OK with you if your boy sleeps over at my place? He'll be safe there. I don't want him in the way.'

She didn't hesitate.

'Of course, if it's not too much trouble. But we really should call the police.'

A look passed between father and son.

'No,' they said in unison.

'How do you like your tea?' Tom said and steered her into the kitchen.

'Strong,' she replied.

Fran Trennery came into the room. She took one look at Libby and another at her husband who was filling the kettle.

'What's going on?'

'That obvious, eh?' Tom asked, turning to her. 'Sit down, love, while I make some tea.'

'You, make tea!' Fran scoffed, but she sat down anyway.

Later in the afternoon, Libby helped Fran peel the potatoes and set the table. She still wanted to call the police but Fran was dead against it, too. Police stations in small country towns had been closed long ago, Tom said. If they were going to get the police, they would have to wait for them to arrive from Melbourne. An event like this would be regarded as a major police operation and it would probably be morning before any rescue was attempted. By then it might be too late.

She went over the plan that Tom and Ashley had put together. She was to take the truck and return to the farmstead, parking the vehicle some distance away, go by foot to the old cottage and attempt to entice the man out into the open. It was risky, but the one consoling factor was that if the man had wanted to kill either Jack or her, he would have done so before now. He'd had plenty of opportunity.

Tom and Ashley would hide near the old stables. When the man came out into the open, they would jump him. It sounded crazy and she'd said as much, but had been silenced by the look that passed between father and son. City girl, the look said.

Dinner passed quietly. They talked about the weather and the new baby due soon, but it was an effort to keep conversation going. Afterwards Tom went into his study and came out with a rifle.

Libby swallowed as she watched him load it and put spare bullets into his top pocket. She told herself this was a man who had dealt with sheep stealing and who knew how guns worked. She thought about Michael and went to Fran to ask if it was too late to phone the other farm to say good-night to him.

Michael was fine. She told him she would see him in the morning. Suddenly it was dark and Ashley was pulling up outside. Libby thought of Jack again, wounded, somewhere in that rundown house. She swallowed, fought back the tears. She had to be strong.

The men left on horseback and after twenty minutes, Fran said it was time for her to go. She kissed her and hugged her and then she was on her own. She drove the truck slowly along the farm road, with the lights off. Her heart thumped in her chest. Why hadn't she insisted on calling the police? This was madness!

Behind the gum trees at the side of the road, the cottage loomed. She turned off the engine and coasted, looking for a sheltered place to park.

Light from the moon helped her to pick her way past the rotting stables. The vehicle that had been parked outside earlier in the day was gone. The place appeared desolated.

It could be a trap! It could also mean that the man had taken Jack with him. The thought almost made her trip over the low cement slab at the threshold to the door. She reached forward to knock, but her hand shook so much it didn't connect with the wood. She drew breath and forced her hand forward again. This time the knock was clear and deliberate.

She backed away and set off at a run towards the stables. Halfway there her boot caught on something and she went sprawling. Her chest hit the ground. Dust rose and went up her nose. Winded, choking, she gasped for breath, but managed to haul herself up. Spluttering and coughing she lurched into the shadow of the stables. In a minute she got air, could breathe again. She waited, but nothing moved, only the blood roared in her ears. The man did not emerge from the house. There was no sound at all.

A faint whistle from her hidden companions jerked her into action. She went toward the door again. Had Jack been taken away? It didn't bear thinking about.

She banged her fist on the wood, but again there was no sound, only the rustle of leaves in a nearby tree. She pushed open the door as Ashley and Tom arrived on her heels. Ashley swung a torch beam around the room. Spiderwebs crossed the ceiling corners, yellowed newspapers were strewn about the floor. A dilapidated folding chair stood in the middle of the room, but there was no sign of Jack. Libby moved down the passage following the feeble light of her shaky pocket-torch.

'Libby!' Ashley whispered. 'Be careful!'

She took no notice. She had to find Jack and find him alive. Nothing was more important than that.

7

The room she entered was empty. Once there had been curtains at the window. Shreds of material now hung motionless in the stale air, the moonlight drifting through the gaps. The next room was also empty, empty of life. Rubbish left by itinerants littered the floor.

She met Ashley and Tom in the passage. They had not found Jack either, although there was evidence of blood, dried and beginning to brown, in a corner, and scuffle marks on the dusty floor as if a body had been dumped there. It turned her stomach.

Libby went outside. Her hands ached from the way she had been clenching them. Where could Jack be? Where had he been taken? Why had he been taken? She wished she'd asked him more questions about his case.

Tom and Ashley followed her.

'We must call the police now,' she said, speaking slowly.

'You're right,' Ashley agreed gloomily.

Reluctant to leave Jack's last-known whereabouts, they conferred in the yard. Libby crossed her arms against her chest. Coldness and fear gripped her body. A noise on what had once passed for the stable roof made her look up. A possum perched himself on a rotting beam and peered down at her, or was he looking at something else?

'Lend me your torch for a moment, Ashley, please,' she asked.

The body lying face down in the stables was unmistakeably Jack's, but the still of the form shot panic clean through her. She made a sound halfway between a strangled sob and a cry. Very gently, she helped Tom turn him over while Ashley held the torch.

Jack was filthy. Dried blood smeared one side of his face from an ugly cut above his eye. Puffy, purpled flesh covered his cheekbone. She could hardly bear to look at him, but he was alive, unconscious, but alive.

'I'll go and get the truck,' she volunteered.

She reached the truck with unsteady legs and eyes wet with tears. As she swung the vehicle on to the property, Tom and Ashley appeared, dragging Jack between them, his head lolling against his chest. She fought back emotion, screwing up her face with the effort.

'Get in the back,' Tom said to her. 'We'll prop him up on you, give him some sort of pillow, eh, love?'

He smiled wanly at her. She clambered on to the tray of the truck and backed herself up against the cabin. Tom and Ashley hauled Jack's body over to her and laid him into her arms.

'Hold him,' Tom told her as his head fell back against her chest like a dead weight, but she didn't need to be told twice.

'Has he . . . do you think . . . '

She couldn't formulate a sentence.

'I think he's been drugged, love.'

'I'll take the horses back,' Ashley offered. 'You two'll be OK, won't you?'

Libby nodded. Tom got into the driver's seat and started the truck. The engine revved. Noise of static rose as the two-way radio crackled into life. She heard Tom talk to Fran, asking her to call the doctor out to the farm. Jack stirred in her arms, mumbled something, but didn't wake.

She pressed her lips to his short dark hair.

'Oh, Jack,' she murmured, 'don't die on me. I love you.'

She loved him? Had she really said that?

The thought took her breath away, the shock of the realisation crystallising everything. Of course she loved him. Perhaps even yesterday, last night — was it only last night when she had told him she didn't love him? She knew she had been lying.

She loved him. She loved Jack

Trennery. She wasn't sure when she had started loving him, if it was in these past weeks or the years before, but in all the time they had been apart she had never stopped thinking about him, wondering what he was doing, missing his easy laughter, his smiling face, his dark brown eyes.

The truck went over a bump and she rocked against his body. She could never tell him she loved him. The age difference between them was too great. A marriage would never work. Tears streamed down her face, dripping on to his head.

'I love you, Jack,' she whispered to the unconscious man, 'I love you.'

Outside the homestead, Tom turned off the ignition. He got out of the vehicle and went over to Fran, silhouetted in the doorway. Putting his arm around her, he talked softly to her. Libby sat very still, treasuring the weight of Jack against her body, the nearness of him, perhaps for the last time.

Then Tom and Ashley came towards her and lifted Jack off her, carrying him into the house. Fran led her to a chair at the kitchen table and placed a small tumbler in front of her.

'Drink up,' she said.

'What is it?' Libby asked numbly.

'Brandy.'

Libby was about to say she didn't drink spirits, but thought better of it. This was not the time to be fussy.

Tom and Ashley set Jack down into a chair across the table from her. Somewhere between the truck and the house he had regained consciousness, but his eyes were glazed. In the bright kitchen light he looked worse, if that was possible. His lips were dry and cracked, the cut above his eye oozed blood, and all around the eye the flesh was bruised and grazed.

'Drink up,' Fran said to her again, coming to the table.

Libby took a tentative sip and grimaced. She watched Fran hold a glass of water to Jack's mouth. Then she wrung out a cloth in a bowl of water and carefully dabbed at Jack's face. He pushed his mother's hand away.

'Oh, Libby, love,' he said his voice cracking, 'what on earth happened to you? Did you fall off the horse?'

The use of the endearment caught her off guard.

'Excuse me?'

The family stopped what they were doing and looked first at Jack and then at Libby. Ashley, snorting with laughter, could hardly get the words out.

'He should talk!'

'What? What is it?'

She rose to her feet and pushed her way across to the oval-framed mirror hanging above the dresser. She was covered in dirt! She'd quite forgotten her fall. Her once pale blue shirt was the colour of the earth. A streak of oil crossed her cheekbone and tell-tale marks of dried tears smeared her face.

No wonder they were laughing, albeit friendly laughter. She felt a flush of heat begin along her neckline. With a bit of luck it would go undetected under the dirt. She smiled wryly.

'I'll just go and clean up.'

Her eyes met Jack's as she left the room. She gave him a little smile. He mouthed something at her, but she put her finger to her lips and shook her head. This was no time for talking, not in front of his family, not if he was going to embarrass her again.

When she returned, the doctor was examining Jack. In his drugged state, Jack kept interrupting. Ashley threatened to remove him from the room if he didn't settle down, but Jack created such a fuss at this the doctor said it would be best if they let him be. He didn't want any stitches coming loose. He said he was very lucky. Any lower and Jack would have lost his eye.

When the doctor had gone and everyone was awash with tea and brandy, Ashley persuaded Jack to have a shower as he was not fit to be in company. Fran and Tom sighed audibly as he went off with his brother, muttering that he'd had a shower less than twelve hours ago, that there was nothing wrong with a bit of dirt.

Libby, barely managing to keep her eyes open, excused herself to go to bed. She'd gone past the stage of wide-eyed excitement. The brandy had seen to that. A look passed between Fran and Tom.

'You can't sleep out there on your own tonight. Have Ashley's old room. The bed's made up,' Fran offered.

Libby was grateful. She fetched her toiletries, nightgown and clean clothes for the morning from the guest quarters, and Tom led her down the passage to the second bathroom. She stripped off her dusty, dirty clothes, threw them into a heap on the floor and ran the water for a long, hot shower.

She didn't even turn on the light in Ashley's room. She found a bed and got into it. It was old but extremely comfortable, but despite being so exhausted she didn't fall asleep straight away. Someone was clattering around in the kitchen. The bedroom door opened and the light went on. She raised her head, blinking in the sudden brightness. There was a considered silence, then the light was extinguished.

'Are you asleep?' Jack asked, sounding more like his normal self.

'Not now.'

He came into the room.

'I needed food and now I'm wide awake.'

'Have you had a hot drink?'

'I've had two glasses of milk, four pieces of toast, some cold lamb and a piece of fruit cake.'

'I'm not surprised you can't sleep!'

'What I really want . . . '

He trailed off and sat down on the edge of her bed. In the light from the passage she could see him staring at her. She rolled on to her side, raised her elbow and propped up her head.

'We need to talk,' she said.

'I know.'

'Jack,' she began.

'Yes?'

She thought he was back to normal, but his breathing was anything but. It sounded ragged. What kind of drug had he been given? The doctor said he should know in twelve hours. Wasn't there anything that could calm him in the meantime?

'Jack, what are you going to do about what happened, about these threats, this case?'

'Oh, that,' he said moodily, cutting her off.

'What do you mean, oh, that? It's important! What are you going to do?'

'Nothing.'

'Nothing?'

'I will do something, but it's not easy. I don't have any proof. Most probably it'll all just die down, once the case is over.'

She sank back down, and lay still, looking at the ceiling.

Why was he still sitting expectantly on the edge of her bed and when would he go away? She began to doze off. It was that blasted brandy!

'Is there nothing else you want to tell me?' he said at last.

He reached out and ran his finger gently down the side of her face. She was instantly alert.

'No,' she said carefully.

There wasn't — or was there?

With his face in shadow, his back to the light in the passage, it was difficult to tell, but she got the distinct impression he was amused by her answer.

'Jack,' she said, rearranging her legs under the covers, 'I'm very tired. Do you mind?'

'I know you are, I'm sorry. I'm tired, too. It's just that . . .'

He left the sentence hanging and walked to the door.

'Good-night, Libby,' he said.

In the morning, when she woke, she couldn't remember where she was. She stared at the ceiling until it all came back to her. Raising herself on one elbow, she reached across to the bedside table for her watch. Her hand stopped in mid-air. Last night the twin bed had been empty. This morning there was a man in it!

Fully clothed, Jack lay on top of the bed, one long leg resting on the floor and bent at the knee as if he had been sitting on the bed, fallen backwards and gone to sleep.

What was Jack doing in the room, and how long had he been there?

She checked her watch. It was half-past ten! She stretched herself, then creeping quietly out of bed, she collected the clean clothes she'd piled at the end of the bed the night before, but he didn't stir. He looked dead to the world.

With her teeth and hair brushed, and dressed in fresh jeans and a pink polo shirt, she felt almost human. In the kitchen she made herself a cup of tea. The homestead was deserted. Sitting at the table still laid with the breakfast things, she found a note propped up against the sugar bowl.

Dad and I have gone to see Marg,

the note said. *I hope you take the time to ring the police in Melbourne. We'll be back later this afternoon. Cold meats for lunch in the fridge. Love, Mum.*

The phone rang, interrupting the complete peace with its shrill sound.

'Hello,' she said hesitantly.

'Good morning. I'd like to speak to Jack Trennery, please.'

'Jack's — '

She faltered. She didn't want to wake him.

'He's not available,' she said. 'May I take a message?'

'Libby Hargraves wouldn't happen to be there, would she?'

'This is Libby. I am Libby.'

This was too early and too soon after the events of the night before for her brain to be functioning properly.

'Nigel Murdoch, Libby. I have good news,' he said.

'You do?'

Jack came into the kitchen as she was winding up the call. He had changed his shirt and had a shave, but he didn't look good. With his stitches and yellowed bruising, he was not a pretty sight at all. Still, she was very glad to see him up and about, and alive. In fact, she was so glad she found it hard to drag her eyes away from him.

'Who was that?' he asked, pulling out a kitchen chair.

'Nigel Murdoch.'

She offered him the coffee pot enquiringly. He held out his cup in answer.

'Did you tell him what happened?'

Libby sank into a chair, reaching for the sugar.

'I didn't need to. He already knew.'

'How? Go on,' he said gently.

'Late last night, a man driving a stolen vehicle was arrested just outside Melbourne. The matter would have ended there, but your wallet was in his pocket.'

'My wallet?'

He automatically patted his hip pocket, a look of dismay on his face.

'I didn't even know it was missing. Did you?'

She took a sip of her coffee and shook her head.

'The police tried to phone you to let you know, but of course you weren't home. They were going to keep trying when they found Nigel's business card in your wallet. I suppose he's fairly well-known because of his rugby connections. In any event, they phoned him on the off-chance he might know where you were.'

She took another sip of coffee.

'When they described the man to Nigel, his suspicions were aroused because the description of the man fitted the one I had given him. He went down to the station and told then about the attack on you, what happened to me in the car and so on. When they confronted this man with all of that, he apparently gave in and confessed he'd had another go at you and abandoned you in the stables.'

'So you would have found me

eventually,' he joked.

'Jack, you might have . . . you might have . . . '

'Died?'

She blinked, lowered her head and fumbled for a tissue.

'The bad news,' she went on after a minute, trying her best to ignore the concerned expression on his face, 'is that the police are on their way.'

'Oh, blast,' Jack said with feeling, putting down his coffee cup. 'I was hoping to have you to myself today. What's the good news?'

'The good news?'

'You said that was the bad news. There must be good news.'

She drew a deep breath. She'd almost forgotten.

'It's about the insurance company,' she said in a rush.

He drew his eyebrows together in a frown, forgetting one was firmly stitched.

'Ouch!' he said.

'You OK?'

'I'm OK,' he replied, giving her a smile.

How could he smile at a time like this?

'What about the insurance company?'

'I haven't had a chance to tell you. I've hardly seen you.'

'Tell me about it,' he interrupted.

She went on.

'Nigel was with Simon the night before the plane crash.'

'With Simon?' he said, incredulous.

'I know, it's weird, isn't it? Pure coincidence. He met him in the hotel where he was staying, at the bar.'

Jack put his head into his hands.

'The bar? Oh, no!'

'Wait, let me finish.'

Jack lifted his head.

'I told you Simon was the sort of man who would talk to anyone. He talked to Nigel, and this is the good bit. Nigel says he didn't drink anything else except orange juice. They went to their rooms together just after midnight and

Nigel's checked with the hotel and nothing was taken out of the room's bar fridge.'

'So he was as sober as a judge, so to speak?'

'Yes, and Nigel's checked with all the air crew, too. They've all sworn blind Simon never drank before a flight, and he certainly hadn't been drinking that night.'

'My apologies, then. I was wrong about him.'

'Oh, Jack,' she said softly.

'So, where does that bring us?'

'It brings us to something else. Nigel's been investigating the insurance company on behalf of another client. He's discovered they've been fobbing off claims, distorting some facts, here and there.'

Jack's eyes widened.

'They only did it to people they thought they could take for a ride. In my case, a single mum, in Nigel's client's case, an elderly woman. There are a few people on their pay list, such as the pathologist who filed the autopsy report and one or two policemen who were bought off for their silence.'

Jack reached for an apple from the fruit bowl and wordlessly bit into the red skin.

'Nigel's client is going to sue the insurance company, but he says he doesn't think that will be necessary in my case. He says we should just send a simple letter, disputing the blood alcohol level, mentioning we have proof Simon was sober. That ought to be enough to warn them we're on to them. They're on their toes, or maybe it's their knees,' she added thoughtfully.

'You and Murdoch have single-handedly solved your problems. I'm impressed. Who needs a lawyer? Anything else?'

'Yes, what were you doing sleeping in my room last night?'

'Your room?' Jack spluttered through a mouthful of apple.

'I mean Ashley's room.'

'Ashley's room?'

'Jack, stop repeating everything I say!'

He grinned. Clearly, he was enjoying himself!

'It's my room, Libby, love. Ashley's old room is across the passage. You were in my bed.'

'Your bed?'

Libby drew breath. She'd slept in his bed! She'd been in his bed when he'd opened the door! What on earth must he have thought? Heat began in her neck and spread to her face. Why had his father led her to Jack's room in the first place? Surely he didn't think . . . She stopped. Tom Trennery hadn't led her to any specific room, he had led her to the bathroom. She had made the decision about the room, if you could call it a decision.

What must Jack have thought!

She frowned. He'd called her that name again, too — love.

'How much time do we have before the police arrive?'

Jack's question cut through the chaos

in her head. She checked her watch.

'Nigel said they left about an hour ago.'

She glanced up at Jack and met his eyes. They were filled with amusement and something else, too, an expression she couldn't fathom.

The noise of a car drawing up in the driveway distracted her.

'It can't possibly be them already, can it?'

8

The policemen came and went efficiently. The man they had in custody was connected to Jack's fraud case though the police wouldn't say how exactly. He appeared to be an amateur, an ex-employee of Waterson's, a man with simply a grudge against Jack's client, taking advantage of the situation, determined to jeopardise Waterson's court case.

The police were tight-lipped, not at liberty to divulge anything further until an extensive investigation had been conducted. Statements were taken from Jack and from Libby, and Ashley was called for. He had time to tell Libby that Michael was fine.

At some stage, they all got into a police car and drove down to the dingy cottage where they re-enacted the drama. Fingerprints were taken. Then they all came back again. Libby found the cold meat in the fridge and made sandwiches, Jack made more coffee. The doctor rang in the middle of it all. He'd just heard that Jack's drug intake was no more than an excess of sleeping tablets.

Finally, they found themselves alone again. Jack looked done in. Libby left him on the sofa and quietly cleared away the remains of the lunch.

'Don't do that now,' he called.

'I must,' she answered. 'Your parents will be back soon.'

He came into the kitchen.

'What can I do to help?'

'Go and have a sleep.'

'I don't want to sleep.'

Knowing better than to argue with him, she passed him a tea towel. When the dishes were done, he stood in the kitchen and waited while she wiped down the sink and hung up the tea towel.

'Finished?'

'Yes,' she said. 'Now will you go and

have a nap. You look terrible.'

'No, I'm not going to have a nap. I want to talk to you.'

'What about?' she said lightly.

Why was he looking at her as if she had done something unspeakable?

'I want to talk to you about you,' he said. 'Come outside. I can't talk to you in the kitchen.'

She didn't want to go anywhere with him. Something in his tone of voice told her it wouldn't be a good idea. Just then, another car drew up in the driveway. Libby peered through the window. It was Tom and Fran returning. She wasn't going to be alone with Jack after all. Help was at hand.

'Oh, no! What does one have to do to get some privacy round here?' Jack muttered.

'Hello!' Libby said, light-headed with relief as Fran came through the kitchen door.

'The police've been' Jack told her tersely. 'They've only just left.'

'We know,' his mother said, passing

through the kitchen. 'We met them on the road just after we left Marg. Be a dear and put the kettle on, please, Libby. I could do with a cuppa after that episode!'

Libby put the kettle on. She found the milk and sugar and laid the tray with four cups. Jack picked up two of the cups and replaced them in the cupboard.

'We are not having tea,' he hissed.

'Yes, we are.'

She put the cups back on the tray.

'Damn it, Libby, I want to be alone with you.'

He picked up the cups again. When he wanted something, he could be very demanding.

'I know. Do you think I'm stupid?'

He put her trembling hands behind her back.

'No, I don't think you're stupid. Nearly all of the time I think you're pretty smart, except for now, when you're stupid. Do you know why?'

'I don't want to know why.'

She shifted her weight from one foot to the other, wondering if she could get past Jack, escape to some place where he couldn't touch her.

'Put the cups back, Jack.'

'All right, have it your way.'

He banged the china down on to the tray.

'There. I've put the cups back. Now what are you doing to do?'

'I'm going to make tea.'

She turned, fumbled with the kettle and swilled hot water into the tea-pot. She heard Jack take a deep breath.

'So you want me to pour out my feelings for you in front of my parents, remembering that I'm thirty years old.'

She halted, the tea-pot poised in mid-air over the sink. He wouldn't really, would he? But how far could she push him?

'Oh, Libby,' he said in exasperation, 'does it really matter how old you are?'

'We've been through this already!' she reasoned.

'We're going to go through it again!' he insisted.

His mother came into the kitchen, silencing them both. She reached for the cake tin and, taking a knife out of the drawer, she cut slices of fruit cake. The air was so thick with tension, she could have cut that, too.

Libby poured boiling water over the tea leaves. Some of the water spilled and went over the tea-pot's edge. Fran, fishing in the cutlery drawer nearby, didn't notice.

'Libby?' Jack broke the silence.

She lifted her face to meet his dark eyes. Between them Fran continued the search for cake forks. His mouth opened, closed. Libby held her breath.

'I love you,' he whispered over his mother's head.

The clink of cutlery ceased abruptly. Libby screwed up her eyes. This wasn't happening, was it? The drawer was pushed in. Cake forks jingled. Footsteps hurriedly receded. A door closed.

'You can open your eyes now, she's gone.'

He stood close, hemming her in against the worktop.

'Oh, Jack, how could you embarrass me and your mother like that!'

'You left me no option.'

He put his arms around her and pulled her against his chest. There was no escape, nowhere else to go.

'When I was lying on the floor, drifting in and out, all I thought about was you,' he said huskily, kissing the top of her head. 'I'm not going to give up on you. I love you, I love you, I love you,' he told her, covering her face with kisses. 'I know you love me.'

She pulled away, studied his face. There were four freckles near his nose she noted, not five as she had thought. How would she know whether nine years would make a difference if she never took a chance to find out?

'Jack, I've only known you for three weeks.'

'Ten years,' he corrected her, his gaze

leaving hers and looking into the distance. 'We've known each other for ten years.'

'What did you say?'

'I said it's been ten years.'

'No, before that.'

'I said I know you love me.'

She frowned. How had he found out she loved him? Suddenly he lowered his mouth towards her, and there were no defences left, no words either. He loved her, completely and utterly. He had been prepared to give up his life for her, throwing himself at the gunman. What did nine years matter? In the scheme of a lifetime together, did nine years amount to much?

In a little while when they were both breathless, he pulled his mouth gradually away from hers.

'Did you know the unconscious mind is able to absorb information and remember it?'

'It is?'

'I'm sure you told me something while I was unconscious. I have this

171

vague picture in my mind of lying in the back of the truck and you're bending over me, telling me something.'

'I am?'

She flushed, lowering her gaze.

'Libby,' he warned, but he was smiling, 'you know what you said. Now tell me again.'

'Gosh, but you are persistent.'

She gazed into his eyes again, loving every part of the man who was Jack Trennery.

'I think I told you I love you. Was that what I said?'

He growled at her and nuzzled his nose into her neck, tickling her until she broke into giggles.

'Tell me again,' he insisted.

She became serious.

'I love you, Jack. I think I've been loving you for years.'

'I know I have,' he said, tilting back her head, looking at her with a fierce longing.

But for Libby, anxiety remained.

'Oh, Jack, do you think it'll work? I'm

so worried about . . . about . . . '

'About me going bald?'

'No!'

'You think you're worried?' he admitted. 'Look at me. I've got to prove myself every day.'

'What do you mean?'

He chuckled nervously.

'I've got to prove I'm not a boy like you said I was!'

Libby reached up and kissed him on the mouth in answer. The kiss deepened as she slid into his arms once more. A sharp rap on the door startled them and they stepped away from each other like guilty teenagers.

'Any chance of getting our tea in the next five years?' Jack's parents called out.

At the close of Jack's case, he took six months' leave of absence from Williams & Nash. He said he'd had enough excitement to last him for years and needed to keep a low profile. While he was keeping a low profile he demolished the old cottage at the farm and built a homestead, solid and sprawling. Libby saw him at the weekends and they loved each other all the more for the time spent apart.

She continued to work for Campbell although she now no longer needed the money, having been paid out in full by the insurance company. Campbell had brought them together again, she insisted at Jack's protests, and she owed him. She was extremely loyal, another of the traits that Campbell and Jack admired in her.

In the spring, they were married. It was a simple ceremony under the flowers of the bougainvillaeas Jack planted outside the new farmstead. Campbell came to the wedding, Libby's parents were there along with Ruth, Ashley and Claire and their new baby girl. Michael and his step-cousins wore elasticated bow-ties which they pulled away from their collars and then let go with great hilarity.

Jack never attended a single law conference without Libby or went overseas on business on his own, for that matter. She always went with him, leaving the children who quickly followed their marriage with one of their grandmothers. She loved him to distraction and couldn't bear to be away from him. They'd been apart too long for them to ever be separated again.

And every wedding anniversary, Jack sent her nine red roses, one for each year of age difference, to remind her that he loved her, regardless.

THE END

CONVALESCENT HEART

Lynne Collins

They called Romily the Snow Queen, but once she had been all fire and passion, kindled into loving by a man's kiss and sure it would last a lifetime. She still believed it would, for her. It had lasted only a few months for the man who had stormed into her heart. After Greg, how could she trust any man again? So was it likely that surgeon Jake Conway could pierce the icy armour that the lovely ward sister had wrapped about her emotions?

TOO MANY LOVES

Juliet Gray

Justin Caldwell, a famous personality of stage and screen, was blessed with good looks and charm that few women could resist. Stacy was a newcomer to England and she was not impressed by the handsome stranger; she thought him arrogant, ill-mannered and detestable. By the time that Justin desired to begin again on a new footing it was much too late to redeem himself in her eyes, for there had been too many loves in his life.